Steamboat
Twisted Tales of Familiar Faces
Courtney Konstantin

M4L Publishing

A Monster in the Shadows

THE HUMIDITY OF THE Arkansas bayou was only made cooler while on the water. Drifting in a boat under the shade of the cypress trees, Jonas dropped his fishing line into the water again. It was one of those afternoons he always enjoyed. He left the house early, before his mother even had the chance to tell him he had chores. Launching his boat from the nearest makeshift dock, he would fish until the sun started to set.

He'd had a little luck so far, with just two fish in his cooler. At first, his mother would be angry that he skipped out on his weekend chores. But once she saw the fish, her mood would lighten. Then she would fry up his catch, and they would enjoy a nice dinner together that she didn't have to pay for.

With that in mind, Jonas lost himself in the line, waiting for a bite, already tasting the delicious fish. He was used to the sounds and sights of the bayou. Not much took his attention away from his task. However, a repetitive creaking sound pulled his eyes from the water. He craned his head, turning his ear toward the sound.

As his boat rounded a bend in the river, he was shocked to find a dilapidated steamboat. It reminded him of the casino boats that were sometimes on the city river ways. He had never been on one, but he and his mother had visited a park that was along the river in the city. While they picnicked, the music of the steamboats pulled Jonas's attention, and his mother explained what was going on. It sounded like they were having a good time.

This steamboat, though, looked like it was slipping into the river. He imagined the inside was slowly filling with water. The main floor, which would normally be well above the water, was practically sitting on the river surface. Spanish moss hung around the railing and the ceiling, hiding the interior. Jonas was immediately struck by the mystery.

This was a part of the river he was well familiar with. He looked around to try and determine if he had gone further than ever before, but he recognized the bend behind him. And he knew he hadn't been in his boat long enough to have gone too far. But the steamboat couldn't have recently been moved. It clearly would have completely collapsed if it had.

Curiosity controlled his movements as he turned on his small motor and putted toward the side of the steamboat. He tied his boat to the side of the wreck and pulled himself through the moss. Without climbing, he found himself mid-ship, on the main deck. The moss closed off the sunlight that was streaming across the river. Jonas realized it felt much cooler. Nerves made him shiver, and he looked over his shoulder back the way he had come.

He moved toward the broken windows that looked into the interior of the boat. Peering through, he was careful not to catch himself on the jagged shards that still sat in the frame. He could imagine parties and dinners being held on the steamboat. There were broken pieces of furniture left inside. Again, Jonas found himself wondering where the boat came from. How it came to be sitting on the riverbed in this area.

He knew it had to be run aground, given how much of the boat was underwater. Jonas made his way further down the decking until he found a black hole in the wood. Leaning over, he could see water below, black as night and completely still. If there were any animals living in the water, they weren't giving themselves away.

A creaking sound from behind him had Jonas spinning around. He could barely see the opening where he had climbed onto the boat. It made him start to walk back. He could hear his mother's voice, telling him this was a bad idea. Any time he climbed a tree that was too high, or he rode his bike without a helmet, he would get a lecture from his mother.

As he walked back toward his boat, he noticed something moving in the shadows at the opposite end of the boat. His imagination conjured alligators, snakes or even a bear. But as the movement continued, it was clear it was too tall to be any of those animals. Jonas froze in fear, feeling as if he was being stalked by an unseen force.

"Who's there?" His voice was shaky and high-pitched. He cleared his throat, not wanting to sound small. "Who's there?!" he called out again.

Out of the shadows, a grumbling laugh bubbled and flowed out over Jonas. He shivered, the malevolence of the sound shooting fear through his body. That fear made him feel as if his feet were glued to the deck. He knew he needed to run. He knew whatever was on the boat with him wasn't something he wanted to face. However, he wasn't able to move an inch.

Suddenly, something that looked like a foot slid into the dim light shining from the opening of the Spanish moss. The leg that appeared a second later turned Jonas's stomach to stone. Long and skeletal, the leg didn't belong to any human Jonas had ever seen. Another leg appeared, and slowly a body was also revealed. The rest of the body was just as skeletal, with patches of dark, decaying flesh hanging, intertwined with the exposed bone.

The head was the most shocking thing, and Jonas couldn't swallow the gasp of surprise that rose up in him. The monster's head was too big for its body, large ears at the top. One of them was partially cut away or had decayed. The eyes that seemed to focus on him were empty pits within the massive face. Jonas couldn't pull his eyes away from the monster and as he stared, the mouth split open in a smile, which flashed impossibly sharp teeth.

Overalls hung from the decomposing body, torn into shreds. Jonas was confused by the fact that it was wearing clothes, even though it wasn't human and likely never had been.

As Jonas stood, frozen in place, the monster moved forward. Its movements were awkward, but quick and threatening. Clawed fingers came up and reached toward the boy, grabbing him and tearing into his flesh. At the pain, Jonas was suddenly shaken from his fear and he screamed. The sound seemed to echo within the steamboat, and it caused the monster to let out another of its low guttural laughs.

"Scream, boy. Scream. There will be no one to come."

Jonas tried to pull away, but the claws only slid into him deeper. The pain was more than anything he had ever felt in his life, and he started to cry. The monster turned and began to drag Jonas along the decking toward the hole he had looked into earlier. As they approached, Jonas was pulled into the monster's body, the spindly bones and rotting flesh wrapping around him.

The last thought Jonas had, as the monster pulled them both into the depths of the steamboat, was that he should have listened and followed his mother's rules.

Reaching Out from Beyond

THE SCREAM THAT RIPPED from her throat caused her to startle awake. Serenity Miller looked around her small bedroom and gave herself a moment to feel oriented. Sunlight was just barely illuminating the room, and she could clearly see that she was alone. There were no monsters hiding in the shadows.

"Itty?" Her best friend and roommate, Daphne, called her silly nickname from the other side of her bedroom door.

"I'm fine," Serenity called back.

"Coffee's on."

Serenity stretched, allowing her tense muscles to release and relax before she rolled out of bed. The nightmares weren't unexpected, though some were harder than others. This one was a rough one. Daphne was used to the screams, talking, and sleepwalking. She knew what haunted Serenity and was always an understanding friend when she woke in the middle of the night.

When Serenity finally left her room in search of coffee, Daphne was heading toward the door with a travel mug in her hand.

"Bad one?" Daphne asked.

"Not anything I haven't had before."

"Want to talk about it?"

Serenity had talked about it for years, since she was a teenager. But talking hadn't helped stop the nightmares. She shook her head. "Have a good day."

Daphne nodded and opened the front door. "See you tonight."

With that, Serenity was alone in their quiet apartment. She made her coffee and leaned against the counter as she sipped the hot liquid. A cup of wake-up was exactly what she needed to make it through her workday. While she enjoyed her coffee, she tried to push her nightmare from her memory.

She had lied to Daphne. The nightmare wasn't the same as she'd had before. And it still sat vividly in her mind. However, it was the same place as it always was. The bayou of Arkansas, where she grew up. She hadn't been home in years, but it was always a moment away in her thoughts. Trauma did that, she assumed.

Leaning into her mirror, she worked on her makeup, determined to get into the office on time and ready to work. Being a sales manager wasn't her life's dream, but it paid the bills and kept her from crawling home to beg Mama or Daddy to let her stay. She would do anything necessary to not go back to that place.

Savannah, Georgia, was the place she called home, and it was the place that made her happy. Walking out to her car, she enjoyed the fall chill in the air. She breathed deep, hoping to wash away the dread in her chest. It wasn't just the nightmare, but also the date that was coming. An anniversary that she wished she didn't have burned into her internal calendar.

Serenity's workday was packed, with calls, meetings, and spreadsheets. It still wasn't enough to help her unease. She was relieved to get home and find Daphne already on the phone, ordering pizza.

Together, they sat at their small coffee table, sharing a bottle of wine and a pizza with every topping possible.

"How was your day?" Daphne's question was an opener, and Serenity knew what she was really asking.

"It's coming up. I think that's why I had such an awful nightmare last night."

Daphne lifted her wineglass and pointed it toward Serenity. "I know the date, that's why I asked. I don't just pop a cork on the good stuff for no reason."

Serenity snorted, almost causing the wine to come through her nose. "The good stuff you opened doesn't actually have a cork."

Daphne just shrugged.

Serenity laid her head back on the couch and sighed. "It's not like I want to remember the anniversary of losing my best friend."

"Or remember how no one believed you about what happened?"

It was just like Daphne to hit the nail on the head. Losing her childhood best friend in a horrific way was one part of the story. The other part was still playing out even as she became an adult, moved away from the bayou, lived her own life. A story of how no one in her small town, population less than a thousand, believed her when she told them what happened to Travis. The boy who she had known since diapers and believed she would marry someday.

When Travis disappeared without a trace, Serenity was the only one with him. She was found bleeding, filthy, and hiding in a tree. When the police discovered her, she screamed, afraid that what took Travis was coming back for her. Sedated, the hospital staff monitored her for days. Her outside wounds were superficial, but her mental damage was beyond repair.

Detectives, therapists, Travis's family, and her own parents questioned her over and over about what happened to him. Despite the state she was in, she was clear about her story. She repeated the same facts over and over. The detectives easily dismissed her as a traumatized child that didn't know fact from fiction. Her own parents looked at her with pity and stopped asking questions. The worst was Travis's mother, who accused Serenity of keeping the truth from them, and not allowing them to put their child to rest.

The story of a steamboat they had never seen, which looked as though it had been sitting in the bayou for decades. How Travis joked and laughed as they both climbed aboard to search the vessel. And how he was never seen again, and she barely escaped with her own life. She tried to tell them she only got away because of Travis. He saved her.

Yet, no matter how much detail she gave them, no one believed her. They assumed Travis, a child of the bayou, drowned in its waters.

After Serenity left the hospital, she led them to the bend where she and Travis found the steamboat. Yet it was gone. The knowledge caused Serenity to have another breakdown, and they sedated her in a hospital bed once more.

Years later, Serenity still had nightmares of the monster of the steamboat. She could never name it. It didn't look like any of the monsters children normally feared. It wasn't a person hiding behind a mask. It wasn't a cryptid, that Serenity had grown up hearing about throughout her childhood.

The police didn't take her seriously enough to use a sketch artist, but over the years, she had drawn what she remembered. It wasn't hard to dredge up the memories of the horrific entity. She'd drawn him many times, and then ripped the images to shreds.

"No one was going to believe a teenage girl that claimed a monster kidnapped her best friend slash boyfriend," Serenity said.

"Well, you said he had overall shorts on with a name tag that read 'Willie,' right?" Daphne said.

That name sent a chill down Serenity's spine.

Serenity had lived out the rest of her high school years depressed and disconnected from anything that a regular teen cared about. She couldn't escape the looks, the whispers, due to her involvement in the mystery surrounding Travis's death. The moment she could leave town, she did. And she didn't look back.

Meeting Daphne while in community college had been an answered prayer. Daphne was wild, fun, and carefree. When Serenity finally told her about her deepest fears and trauma, her friend didn't blink. She accepted Serenity and her story without hesitation. It was the first time anyone validated her experience. She understood that this validation came from someone who hadn't lived through the loss of Travis and its effect on their community. But it didn't matter. Someone believed her.

"These dreams, the last few I've had, are different. Usually, they're just the memories of what I saw. The moment that I was grabbed by the creature, his claws digging into my flesh. And Travis jumping into action. It always ends with me watching as Travis is dragged away, screaming and begging for me to run," Serenity said.

"So how are these new ones different?"

"I see Travis in the moments after I ran. I watch as he's tortured by the monster and then drowned in the bayou. But the worst part is, Travis speaks to me." Serenity felt the goosebumps rise along her body. Her friend's voice was clear in her mind, even years later. He sounded no different in her dreams.

"Maybe your mind is creating something to comfort you? To make you feel like he's alive?" Daphne lifted her wineglass to her mouth and peered at Serenity over the rim.

"After all this time, my subconscious suddenly wants to make something up for me? That seems weird. Nothing has changed recently."

"Okay. What else are you thinking? I can see the wheels turning."

Serenity shifted uncomfortably on the couch, looking away as she answered. "What if Travis is reaching out to me?"

The Steamboat's Call

Daphne let her debate her thoughts, rolling around everything that had been in her mind since her nightmares changed. By the time Serenity's eyelids were drooping, she was no closer to understanding what was happening. Daphne said goodnight, and they went to their rooms.

Serenity wanted to avoid sleep. There was a sinking feeling in her chest that she would dream of them again. Willie and Travis. She hoped she'd dream of Travis, where he looked healthy and whole, laughing as they climbed aboard the abandoned steamboat. But those dreams were rare. She more often remembered how Travis looked when he was taken from her. Scared, bleeding from multiple wounds, and screaming her name.

She pushed the memory away, not wishing for it to infect her sleep. In her bathroom, she poured a pill into her hand. Sleeping pills had been part of her routine for years. Falling asleep was the hardest part, but she couldn't control what happened once she did.

After following her evening ritual with a fan, fuzzy socks and a sleep meditation playing, she curled up on her side. The wine, along with the exhaustion from her day, made her drowsy. Sleep didn't hesitate to wash over her. However, it wasn't the darkness she had hoped for.

Almost immediately, Serenity found herself in the bayou. She didn't immediately panic, because sometimes she dreamed of the happiness she had experienced there as a child. Travis was there for those dreams too, but he was younger and always happy and alive.

"Serenity," a voice came from behind her.

She was sitting in a rowboat, but she wasn't manning the oars. When she turned, she found Travis. His movements were slow and deliberate as he pushed their boat down the river. He was a teenager, and the panic rose in Serenity. Her dream mind didn't know why she felt panic and fear. Instead, she felt affection bloom in her heart.

"Where are we going, Travis?" She turned and looked forward as they glided through the water.

"You know, Ser."

He was the only one to shorten her awkward name. Growing up in a small town of Brendas, Lisas, and Corys, Serenity always felt out of place. But Travis gave her a nickname, so she could feel like everyone else.

"I don't remember," Serenity replied.

She turned back to look at Travis again, and her hands shot to her face, smothering a scream that bubbled up in her throat. The smile on Travis's face was gone. A wide hole replaced his smile, stretching his mouth abnormally, as if he was frozen in a constant scream. Blood streamed from wounds crisscrossing his face. Travis's clothing was torn, filthy, and dripping with water.

Serenity squeezed her eyes shut against the horror and rocked in her seat. Her mind couldn't comprehend what she was seeing.

"Ser?" Travis's voice was soft as he called out to her.

It took all of her courage to force her eyes open and look at her friend again. The sun shone down on his dirty blond hair, creating a halo effect. The blood and gore were gone, his sweet smile back on his face, and his arms moving as he continued to work the oars. Her heart pounded so hard she thought it would burst from her chest, and she couldn't speak.

If she didn't feel the cold sweat trickling down her back, she would have thought she somehow imagined it. But the fear caused adrenaline to course through her veins and her body was feeling the aftereffects of that. Facing forward, Serenity tried to ignore the pull to glance over her shoulder again and again to check that Travis looked normal.

They were approaching a bend in the river and the trepidation in Serenity increased, but she couldn't be sure why. They cruised down the water in many canoes, kayaks, and boats. The same stretch of bayou passed her without changing, except with the seasons. But now, something was screaming at her to stop and go back.

"Travis, maybe we shouldn't go so far today?"

He didn't respond. The boat continued to move, and Serenity just sat in silence. Part of her knew something was around the corner and it was the last thing she wanted to see. But her mind couldn't pull on the string of memory, so she could clearly see the danger. Travis seemed oblivious to any threat. His smiling face tilted up toward the sun.

As they rounded the bend, a sudden disturbance from the shore made Serenity jump in her seat. A river hawk furiously screeched at them as they interrupted its feeding on whatever fish it had caught. The bird flew above the trees and circled overhead, giving Serenity the feeling of being watched. It was unnatural, the way it continued to move above them, even as they completed the turn.

The moment Travis pushed the rowboat straight down the river, Serenity's fears rose, making themselves known. A decrepit boat sat, partially sunk, against the riverbank. It was a medium-sized steamboat, which may have once been used for evening river cruises. Though no cruise like that would go so deep into the bayou. Silvery-gray strands of Spanish moss hung from the roof, hiding much of what was inside the main deck.

"Let's go explore, Ser."

A knot formed in her stomach, and everything inside her told her going near the vessel was a bad idea. But when she looked back at Travis, his face was serene, without a worry. She pushed her feelings aside and tried to be brave. There were no doubts in her mind that Travis would keep her safe, just as he had for so many years of their friendship.

Their boat slid alongside the steamboat, and Serenity wondered if the rotting deck could even hold either of their weight.

"I'm not sure this is safe, Travis."

"Oh, come on, Ser. When weren't you up for a little adventure?"

The feeling of being watched washed over her again. Craning her head, she didn't see the river hawk above them, yet she could feel eyes on her. Something wasn't right, and just as she was going to say something to Travis, he appeared on the main deck, parting the moss for her. She didn't know when he'd climbed aboard, but he held out his hand to her, his winning smile plastered on his face.

The rotting old wood groaned under their footsteps. Serenity placed her feet carefully, watching each movement. She waited for a board to fall away, to cause them to fall to what had to be water below.

"How do you think it got here? I haven't seen a boat like this so far from a big city. It doesn't belong here." Serenity's quiet words rang loud in the cocoon of decaying wood and Spanish moss.

"Maybe it's magic. Woooooo," Travis replied with a small laugh while wiggling his fingers at her.

"Oh, stop it." Serenity had to laugh at his antics, as she smacked his hand away from her.

They continued to move toward the bow of the boat, passing broken windows that revealed the inside was falling apart just as badly as the outside. Something scurried by, only visible for a quick moment in the limited gray light that shone through. Serenity shivered, as if the small creature had crawled up her spine.

A sound from behind them stopped her short, though Travis continued forward. She turned, peering into the gloom, but she saw nothing. Another creaky footstep in the dark made her take a step backward. The shadows seemed to shift as something took shape.

Serenity had seen enough. She turned on her heel and looked for Travis, but she was alone. Her gaze flew around, looking through the broken windows and further down the main deck. Travis had disappeared. The sounds behind her were definitely footsteps, and she didn't want to wait and find out who was coming out of the dark.

Rushing forward, she forgot the careful placement of her feet. Rounding the bow of the boat, she didn't realize until too late that the boards had rotted away. The last thing she saw before falling into darkness was Travis's face, fear etched on his features, as he watched her go down.

The water was shocking to her as she splashed into the flooded underbelly of the steamboat. When she surfaced, she was gagging and coughing up the sludge that entered her mouth.

"Travis!" she screamed.

Serenity had never been a fan of the water. Though she had grown up around it, been on it plenty, she didn't like to be in the water unless she had no choice. She kept her head above the surface, trying to examine the space she was caught in while treading water. It was as she thought. The entire lower deck was flooded, and the bottom of the boat was likely resting on the river floor.

It was almost pitch black in the water, with only some gray light filtering through the hole she'd fallen through. She tried to find anything to grab onto, but whatever wood her hands found crumbled and couldn't support her weight. Her breathing became quick and erratic. Looking up through the hole, she couldn't see Travis and couldn't understand why he had abandoned her.

Movement to her left made her spin in the water. Several predators crowded her mind, and she wondered if she was going to be attacked by a gator before she drowned. She didn't see any telltale signs of the animal, but the water moved as something came toward her.

Leaving the safety of the circle of light, Serenity moved backward, afraid of what was coming for her. Suddenly, something broke through the surface of the water. It wasn't an alligator. It wasn't anything she had ever seen before. Her mind couldn't comprehend what was rising out of the water. A grotesque being that couldn't possibly be real. And it was then she screamed.

Lunch Break Nightmare

The anniversary of Travis's death was looming less than two weeks away, and Serenity could barely keep her focus on work. She checked and rechecked a spreadsheet formula that wasn't working. It was one she had used multiple times in the past, but she couldn't wrap her mind around it. Her focus on her nightmares and past drained her mental energy, making it hard to concentrate on the future and her healing journey.

The numbers swam in front of her exhausted eyes, and she took the loss. Saving the report, she closed it out. She cleared her inbox of anything that needed her attention. She moved things around on her desk, even though it was pristine. A yawn hit her suddenly, and she covered her mouth with her hands. Rubbing her face, she couldn't fight the exhaustion that was ever present.

It was around lunchtime, so she felt safe to close her office door and take a quick break for herself. Serenity often packed her lunch, but she couldn't muster up an appetite. Sitting back at her desk, she laid her head down on her folded arms and let her eyes drift shut. She just needed a few minutes or she wouldn't be able to continue for the rest of her day.

"Ser."

Her eyes snapped open and where she expected to see the four plain walls of her office, Spanish moss surrounded her. The edges of her vision were blurry, not allowing for her to look beyond the moss. However, she didn't need to see anything to know where she was. The steamboat.

"Ser..."

"Travis?" Her voice was barely above a whisper, but there was no need to speak louder, as he was standing directly in front of her.

He looked as he did the last moment she saw him, covered in mud and blood. His hair dripped water endlessly onto his bloody shirt. There was a large gouge in his cheek, where she could almost see through. Strips of his T-shirt were ripped away from the front, and claw marks scarred his pale chest. The wounds leaked blood still, flowing down his body and puddling around his feet.

When Serenity looked down, she tried to step back from the spreading blood, but she was stuck in place. The red continued toward her, flowing over her sneakers and moving around her like a river.

"Ser..."

Her head snapped up, and she looked at Travis again. His eyes pleaded with her, staring into her, as if he could reach out and touch her at that moment. Tears blurred her vision as she stared at her first love, lost for years after saving her from the monster that had murdered him.

"Travis, I'm so sorry."

"You left me, Ser." His words came out garbled as he tried to speak with his injured face.

"I didn't want to, Travis. I tried to help you. But...but...it took you." Serenity's words ended with a sob.

Travis tilted his head back, and his mouth opened wide, letting out a horrible wail, full of pain and fear. Serenity's hands flew up to cover her ears, but the sound was inside her mind, stabbing at her consciousness. It felt like an eternity when the sound stopped, but she didn't move her hands away or open her eyes.

"You need to come back, Ser. Only you can come back. He wants you."

His words were soft now, almost loving. Serenity felt a caress across her cheek, the warmth of his touch across her skin. But her mind knew that wasn't possible. Travis no longer had warmth, no longer had life. He only had his death in the bayou. His body disappearing with the steamboat.

Slowly, Serenity straightened, pulling her hands from her ears. At the last moment, she opened her eyes. Travis no longer stood in front of her. In his place stood Willie, wearing tattered overalls, his name sewn into the pocket. In the brief moments she had seen him, she couldn't determine what type of creature he was. Although his body was shaped like a human, his claws were long, thick and sharp as razors.

His head was what Serenity couldn't understand. It was large and bulbous, too big for his body. His large ears reminded her of a mouse. One ear was tall and round, but the other had been chopped, leaving only half of it.

In the seconds it took Serenity to take in all these features that had haunted her for years, Willie's mouth opened into a wide sharp-toothed grin, drool slowly leaking from one side.

"Come bacccccck." His words were thick and unnatural, ending in a growl.

The monster raised his hands, reaching toward her with clawed fingers. Serenity screamed and tried to step back. Instead of her foot falling onto a wood plank of the deck, she toppled backward into the darkness, her scream echoing in the emptiness.

Serenity startled awake, shooting up in her office chair. The hair that had escaped her bun was plastered to her damp skin. Looking at the clock, she could see she only dozed off for just over ten minutes. But that was all it took for Travis or Willie to pull her back into a nightmare.

It was just like the others she told Daphne about. Travis, talking to her, asking her to come back. As if she could find him and save him. Logically, she knew that wasn't possible. Her heart didn't care about the logic. For years she avoided home, the bayou, her family and everyone that knew about what happened to her and Travis. But now, she didn't think her nightmares would stop until she went back.

Standing up, she shook off the sleepiness and distracted herself with work. The niggling in her mind about the nightmare didn't completely go away, but she could pull up her spreadsheet and correct the formulas she knew like the back of her hand. She worked on two more sets of numbers, speeding through the work she hadn't been able to finish before lunch. After she saved her work, it was almost the end of the day, so she packed up.

At home, Serenity found the apartment empty. For a moment she debated going to the grocery store, so she didn't have to be alone. But the feeling passed. The fear made her feel silly, even though she could vividly remember the nightmare she'd had that afternoon. She moved around her room, separating her clothes and putting things on her bed, with little thought.

Daphne knocked on the doorjamb, startling Serenity out of her mindless activity. When her friend walked in the door, she looked around the room.

"Going somewhere, Itty?"

Her question confused Serenity, but when she looked down on her bed, she found something that surprised her even more. Her old duffel bag, pulled from the very back of her closet, was open, stuffed with clothes. She searched her mind, trying to remember when she made the decision to pack.

"I'm not sure," she replied.

Daphne walked into the room, pulling the duffel wide open so she could look inside. Serenity could see what was packed, and it appeared to be a full wardrobe for at least a week. She couldn't remember touching any of the pieces of clothing that were inside the bag. It was as if her body moved and completed the task without her knowing it. Glancing over at the clock on her nightstand, her skin prickled when she saw an hour had passed since she arrived home.

Her friend just stood and watched her as she tried to figure out what was happening. The nightmare in her office pushed her toward the belief that she needed to go home, needed to figure out what happened to Travis. It was as if he was asking her to find him, but all she'd be able to find was his remains. Maybe he was asking her to put him to rest.

"I think I need to go back. Back home."

The Weight of Home

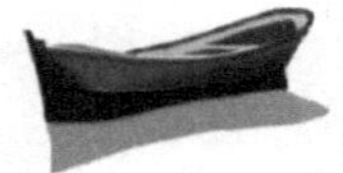

SERENITY STOOD OUTSIDE HER childhood home, a small three-bedroom, ranch-style house that looked as if it hadn't been updated since the 1960s. The discolored brick exterior was covered in moss that crawled up around the base of the house. The porch roof had seen better days. Serenity could see a blue tarp covering what must have been a hole right above the front door.

She could have rented a room in a larger town nearby. After all, she planned to go to the library one county over to research the steamboat and Willie. But something in her heart wouldn't allow her to come this close to home and not stop and see her parents.

They talked once every few weeks. They would ask about Savannah and her job; she would ask them about their pets. They never talked about anything more serious than how her mother was helping care for the old neighbor who had gout. That was southern hospitality. Her mother would lecture. That lecture usually ended with a side comment about how other children always came home to see their parents.

Steeling herself, she walked toward the front door. It was the first time she had come back, and she wasn't sure if she was supposed to just walk in. Was this still her home? She decided on knocking, so she didn't scare her mother if she was home alone. Her knuckles rapped quietly on the front door, since the doorbell was hanging from wires on the wall.

"I'm not buying anything you're selling!" Her mother's shrill voice came through the door before she swung it open.

Serenity wore a nice pair of jeans and a trendy off the shoulder sweater, her attempt at letting her parents know she was doing fine living away from home. She had artfully swept her dark hair into a simple, messy bun, creating a look that was both fashionable and casual. The look on her mother's face told her she had accomplished her goal, but maybe too well. She looked at her daughter as if she didn't recognize her.

"Hi, Mama."

"Serenity? That you? Looking like the city just poured you out on my porch. Well, you gonna come in?" Without another look, her mother disappeared into the house, leaving the door open for Serenity to decide about walking in or leaving.

She took a deep breath and walked through the door, transporting herself to her high school years. A time that she wanted to just forget and never repeat. However, here she was, pushing the door closed and following in her mother's wake. In the kitchen, she found her mother picking up a cigarette she had left in a glass ashtray. She turned and leaned against a counter and studied Serenity through the smoke hovering around her.

"I was wondering if I could stay a few nights. There are some things I need to do, and I thought I could come see you and Daddy while I was here."

Her mother gestured toward the hall that led to her bedroom and the bathroom she had used all her life. Her bedroom and an extra room were located down a hallway off the living room. On the opposite side, another hallway led to the main bedroom where her parents slept. When she was little, she would cry for her parents after having a nightmare, but no one could ever hear her. She had learned to protect herself from the monsters.

"Your room is in the same place. Feel free. This is still your home, Serenity, even if you never come for a visit," her mother said.

It was just like her mother. Welcome her home, but be sure to give her a bit of a dig at the end. Serenity barely held in the sigh that was rising in her chest.

Instead, she plastered on what she hoped was a placating smile and nodded. "Thanks, Mama. I won't be any trouble. And it should only be a few days."

"Stay as long as you need." Her mother turned away to stab out her cigarette. But as Serenity went to walk out of the kitchen, her mother called over her shoulder, "You aren't bringing any trouble home, are ya?"

Serenity knew she couldn't tell her mother that she was back because of dreams. Or that she believed Travis was calling to her through them. She couldn't admit that she was back in town to find the Steamboat. Her mother would never understand.

It took little for her to remember how her parents used to ignore her in their home because she would not deny her reality, refusing to back down from her version of what had happened to Travis. They would eat meals in absolute silence and that was only on the off chance they were all at the table together. Most nights, Serenity would come from her room in the evening to find a plate for her in the microwave, but her parents had already eaten.

The feeling of abandonment choked her as she put on a fake smile and turned to meet her mother's gaze. "Of course not, Mama. Just tying up some things. I promise to not be a bother to you or Daddy."

Her mother nodded and disappeared down the hall toward her own room. Serenity turned and made her way down the worn carpet to her room. Even her door looked exactly the same, as if her parents had never come down the hall. Stickers, postcards from faraway places, and a Do Not Enter sign remained taped to its surface.

Inside, Serenity flicked on the one-bulb light that hung in the middle of the room. Though everything looked exactly the same, her mother had kept her bed fresh. The blanket and sheets were clean and smelled faintly of the borax homemade laundry detergent her mother always made. There was no dust on her small desk or dresser. That her mother cleaned her room on a normal basis, even when she did not know she was going to visit, did something to Serenity's heart.

She took a moment to unpack her duffel, tucking her clothes into her empty dresser. In the top drawer, she found her old diary. On the outside, in black Sharpie, she had written her first name with Travis's last name over and over. After he died, she never opened the journal again. The dreams for her future had died with him.

Her bed was the same old twin mattress she had slept on until she fled the old ranch-style house. But when she sat down, nostalgia filled her, more than just the need to find the Steamboat. It was about the childhood she had lost and what she had walked away from when she had no other options.

Lying down, she rested her head on her pillow and let her eyes drift shut. Sleep swallowed her quickly and the sunlight of her dream lit up behind her eyelids. When she opened her eyes, she was once again in a canoe, floating down the river. Immediately, she twisted so she could see Travis behind her. He smiled at her, as if he had no worries in the world.

"Hi, Ser."

"Hi, Travis."

"You're home." His words were matter-of-fact, as if he were watching her from whatever heaven he lived in now.

"You told me to come back, didn't you?"

Darkness crept across his face, and the sun disappeared, leaving nothing but shadows between them in the canoe.

"Travis?" Serenity's voice trembled.

"I need you, Ser. But I didn't call for you to come back. He did."

"He? Do you mean Willie? Willie wants me to go back?"

"You escaped him. He doesn't let anyone escape. Now, I'm trapped. Until you come back and take my place." Travis's voice sounded far away, no longer at the other end of the canoe, but somewhere in the bayou beyond.

"How are you trapped, Travis? Your body? Are you alive?" Serenity asked, though she knew the answer. There was no way he was alive all these years, living in the Steamboat with Willie.

Travis made a scoffing noise. "You know that's not what I mean, Ser."

She shook, and cold sweat beaded at her brow. "What do I have to do, Travis?"

"Set my soul free, Ser. I can't exist like this any longer. Set me free..."

Her shoulder was being shaken, and Serenity opened her eyes to find her father looming over her.

"Wake up, girl. And tell your parents why you're really here."

Call of the Bayou

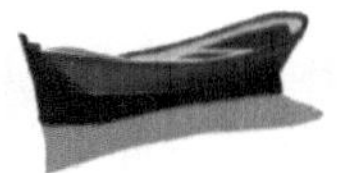

SERENITY FOUND HER FATHER in the living room. He was a large man, tall and round in the middle. The roundness had slightly increased since the last time she had seen him. But to her, he had always been the one to clean her scraped knees, hug her through tears and help her study.

Now he stood with his burly arms across his chest as he watched her warily. It reminded her that the hugs and laughter had ended once her parents didn't believe her about Travis. There was no hug being offered, only judgment and suspicion. Serenity was regretting not just booking a hotel room.

"Hi, Daddy."

"What brings you home?" He didn't bother with pleasantries, getting right down to the issue at hand.

"Like I told Mama, I just have a few errands to run locally. I won't cause any trouble. I just thought I'd come see you both while I was here. Maybe find the chance to visit."

Her father glanced over his shoulder at his wife, who was smoking in the kitchen again. She raised her eyebrows at him, as if telling him to do something. The man sighed and turned back to his only child.

"It took a long time for life to get back to normal here, after, ya know? It wasn't until you went to the city that people stopped looking at us funny. Your mama finally got invited back to her quilting club.

I'm not gonna sugarcoat it, you being back isn't going to be good for us."

After the years she had been away, and even the years of isolation before, she was surprised that her father's words actually hurt her. She knew she wouldn't get a celebration for returning. But she hadn't expected to be told she wasn't welcome. Tears stung, and she took a deep breath to keep herself from falling apart.

"I'm sorry. I'm not trying to bring problems to you. I'll pack my things and get a hotel room."

Without another word from her parents or herself, she spun and rushed back to her room. She didn't worry about packing in an organized manner. She threw all the clothes from her dresser into her duffel. At the last moment, she took her diary as well.

Holding her duffel at her side, she looked around her old room. When she had left the first time, part of her believed she would always be back. Now, she knew it was the last time she would see the room she grew up in. If her parents knew the real reason she was back, the results would be even more dramatic. They would never forgive her for reopening the wound of Travis's disappearance and her story of the mysterious steamboat.

When she came back into the living room, neither of her parents were present. They weren't even willing to tell her goodbye. She knew better than to hope they would ask her to stay. They had made up their minds. The life they wanted to live in the small town next to the bayou was more important than the daughter they believed had mental health issues.

Once she was in her rental car, she let the tears slide down her cheeks. The house blurred in her vision for a moment, before she swiped at her face and threw the car into reverse. Her eyes stayed on the road, without even glancing back at the home she would never see again.

She wove her way out of town, taking a longer route, to avoid seeing Travis's old house. His parents didn't live there anymore. After their son disappeared, they couldn't stomach being around people who wouldn't stop talking about the loss. It hadn't helped them that Serenity had stuck to her story, insisting a monster in the bayou had taken him.

Without meaning to, she found herself at the small dirt shoulder where teenagers would park to launch their boats into the river. Someone had built a small dock, and over the years, the ground into the water had been flattened by all the people that passed by there with their boats. It was the place she and Travis had gone to push their canoe out for a sunny day paddle.

Serenity pulled the car over and stepped out. There was only one other car pulled off the road, but no one seemed to be around. The smell of muddy earth and stagnant water combined to create a familiar aroma. It used to be a smell that comforted and brought her peace. Now, her heart thundered in her chest as she made her way toward the water.

As soon as the water came into sight, Serenity froze in the shade of a bald cypress tree. Her hand came up to rest against the trunk of the tree, trying to stabilize herself. The water seemed completely still until an egret broke the surface as it landed. She watched the bird as it moved around on its long legs and preened. It stretched its neck long and stood still, staring down into the water. She had seen this behavior many times while growing up, but Serenity was still surprised when the bird speared a small fish with its sharp beak.

Watching the egret had helped calm her nerves. Nothing attacked it. There were no boats, real or ghostly, in sight. The bayou looked as it always had, before the nightmare day. Peaceful and beautiful, teeming with life, with something fascinating to watch each moment. The sun filtered through the taller bald cypress that grew off the shore and into the center of the waterway.

Being this close to the place she and Travis had shared as children made her feel closer to him. It was as if his soul could float in the streaming sunlight, watching over his favorite spot.

"I'm here, Travis. Now what?" she murmured to herself.

A few hours later, she had checked into a small hotel that included a free breakfast service. She pushed thoughts of her parents from her mind and thought about how it was much more convenient for her to be close to the library. And the larger town was further from the river, helping her avoid the pull of the water.

Serenity debated whether to take her sleeping medication, unsure if it helped or hurt with her nightmares. Instead, she bought a bottle of wine and had a couple of glasses in her room. She was feeling warm and relaxed when she curled up in bed. The hotel bed wasn't the most comfortable thing she had ever slept on. However, the wine did its job, and she fell into a peaceful sleep, though it wasn't meant to stay that way.

Serenity stood at the edge of the bayou, fog shrouding the water and trees. The air was thick with humidity and the familiar scents of rotting wood and foliage. The sky overhead was starless, and there was no moon to illuminate the river. Unseen creatures rustled nearby, causing a shiver to run down Serenity's spine.

"Ser..."

"Travis?" Serenity spun in place, trying to find the source of Travis's voice.

Her heart raced as she searched for her friend, hoping to see his face. She wanted to see him the way he was before Willie got him. But as his form appeared, and the fog slowly moved away, her heart shattered to see him gray and bleeding. His ghostly hands reached out toward her.

"Release me, Ser. You need to come back and release me."

"Where, Travis? I'm here. But how do I find you?"

The fog seemed to swirl around him, and he disappeared again. Before Serenity could call out to him, the skeletal image of Willie appeared in his place. His face was horrific with sunken, hollow eye sockets, and no pupils visible. The mouth was full of jagged, sharp teeth that Serenity could plainly see in the horrible smile on his face.

"Join us, Serenity. Your friend belongs to me and soon you will too."

Willie's laughter echoed around Serenity. She could feel it vibrate in her chest and she wrapped her arms around herself. Through his wild chuckles, she could hear Travis screaming. The sound he made was filled with fear and pain, begging for Serenity to save him from the hell he was trapped in.

For a moment Serenity saw Travis again and with all the courage she could muster, she launched herself forward, reaching for him. His hands, crusted with blood and mud, reached toward her as well. But just as her fingers were about to graze his, the fog thickened, closing in around her and cutting off her vision.

Serenity's scream didn't leave the fog. She collapsed to her knees, digging her fingers into the mud. With the touch of the earth, she tried to ground herself and remember where she was. As she crouched, the wind swirled around her, lifting her hair from her shoulders. She screamed again, but it still sounded hollow.

Just as she thought she was going to be torn from the ground into the tornado of air, the fog ahead of her parted and the outline of the decaying steamboat appeared. On the bow, she could see the image of Travis still reaching out for her.

"Help me, Ser!" he cried out.

As she watched, Willie's image materialized behind Travis, and the dark depths of the steamboat pulled her friend back in. Serenity cried out, reaching toward the steamboat as it disappeared behind a wave of fog once more.

When Serenity startled awake in her hotel room, her cheeks were damp with the tears she had cried. The nightmares were becoming more vivid, and her body had a hard time telling the difference between what was real and what was a dream. Her heart couldn't seem to slow down, even as she watched the window slowly lighten with dawn's first rays.

Truth Beneath the Surface

SERENITY WAS OUTSIDE THE library before it opened. Drinking coffee from a local café, she stood waiting for someone to open the front door. When the male librarian smiled at her through the glass door, she forced a smile onto her face. She didn't want to give off vibes of someone trying to track down a monster that haunted the bayou.

She tossed her empty coffee cup and stepped into the air-conditioned library. From home she had done some preliminary research, figuring out where the information she needed might be. First stop, local paper archives. She never heard stories or rumors of anyone disappearing the way Travis had. But she was willing to bet he wasn't the first.

After speaking with the librarian, Serenity found herself in a small room with a microfilm machine and rolls of film. The librarian said they had many more years, but Serenity started before she and Travis were born. News travelled fast in their small community, so if someone had gone missing, they would have heard about it. The librarian had asked if he could help her find something specific, but she really wasn't sure how to explain what she was searching for.

It felt like a needle in a massive statewide haystack, but she didn't feel like she could just give up. If she was going to find the steamboat and Travis, she needed clues to what Willie was and where to look. She read through the headlines, film after film, knowing any stories about a missing person, child or otherwise, would be on the front page. There was plenty of crime in the area and several drownings. She took the time to read those articles in depth and found the follow-up stories. None of them mentioned a steamboat or witnesses that could have reported about it.

Stretching her arms above her head, Serenity let out an enormous yawn. The door behind her opened, and she jumped, turning to see a woman peering inside.

"Oh, I'm sorry, dear. I didn't mean to startle you."

"It's okay."

Instead of walking out and closing the door like Serenity expected, the woman came into the room and glanced over Serenity's shoulder. She was an older woman, with gray hair pulled into a bun. Some of the hair escaped and curled around her temples. She was so close to Serenity that she could smell her light floral perfume.

"Drowning? Forty years ago? That's interesting," the woman said as she leaned back out of Serenity's personal space.

She didn't respond to the woman's comment, not sure what she could really say. The woman leaned back and studied Serenity's face.

"I know you, don't I?"

Serenity turned and faced the screen fully, uncomfortable with the scrutiny. She hadn't accounted for the fact that during the years after Travis's disappearance, her picture was plastered across numerous local newspapers. First, it was because she was a survivor and people would comfort her in school and on the street. Then it was to call her a liar, for withholding information from the police that would have led to Travis. Last, it was on the anniversary of his disappearance; she was mentioned again as the lone survivor who had lost her mind.

"I don't think we've met," Serenity replied.

"No, I'm sure I've seen you somewhere. Are you famous or something?"

Serenity shook her head. "Definitely not. Maybe I just have one of those faces."

To dissuade the woman from continuing, Serenity turned off the machine and started changing out film rolls. But there was no sound of the door opening. The woman continued to crowd her space.

"You're the survivor, the crazy girl." The woman's voice was hushed, but Serenity didn't miss a word. The familiar shame flushed her cheeks pink, and she fought to keep her head held high.

"What are you doing back here? I thought you left and were determined to leave this all behind?" The woman paused and then she gasped. "You're looking for the steamboat, aren't you?"

Serenity froze and stared at the blank monitor in front of her. She could vaguely see the woman's reflection, and she focused on it. The woman was covering her mouth with her hand, as if in shock. But she didn't leave and didn't speak further. She just waited for Serenity to do or say something.

"So you read some newspaper articles about me. Good for you. I don't need to explain myself." Serenity's tone was biting, and she was proud of herself for feeling strong.

"Oh, my dear, you misunderstand. I'm not asking for an explanation. And I didn't just read the articles about you. I saved them. I followed them for years. Because, dear girl, I believe you."

The words threw a cold bucket of water on Serenity's annoyance. She now turned to look up at the woman, her eyes round with surprise.

"You believe me?"

The woman nodded her head vigorously. She moved and sat in the empty chair next to Serenity and turned so they were facing each other.

"Yes. Travis was your friend's name, right?" Serenity nodded, and the woman continued. "Travis wasn't the first one. And what I'm sure no one has told you is that he wasn't the last either."

"What?" Serenity's brain was having a hard time keeping up with this new information. She had wanted to believe he wasn't the only one. But no one had told her there had been other disappearances. How could her parents not see those stories and realize Serenity wasn't crazy? How could they still turn her away, knowing others had the same story she did?

"Other people, mostly teenagers having fun, have gone missing on the bayou. You have the regular, still tragic, drownings. Maybe someone drunk falling from their boat. Or someone getting tangled while swimming and they weren't wearing proper gear. But there have been others."

"Has anyone talked about the steamboat?"

The woman tilted her head in thought, then shook it no. "But there was a story about a monster. And the teen boy that saw him called him Willie."

Serenity went cold and bile tried to fight its way up her throat. "Willie?"

"The boy described him as a skeletal monster, with an abnormal head, ears almost like a mouse. He said one of his ears was—"

"Half missing," Serenity said, cutting off the woman.

"Yes."

Serenity covered her face with her hands, shaking her head in disbelief that this was happening still. And she had no idea. She had returned with the conviction that she needed to free Travis from whatever prison Willie had his soul in. She had never expected there to be active stories about the monster.

"I'm Evelyn."

Serenity slowly lowered her hands. "Serenity."

"I know," Evelyn said with a sad smile.

Evelyn suddenly stood and held up her finger as if to say one minute, before disappearing through the door. She didn't close it behind her, and Serenity watched after her. When she came back, she had a large book, and she spread it out on the open table in the small room. Serenity stood to look and realized it was newspapers from the last few years.

Flipping through pages, Evelyn ran her fingers over the dates, until she found what she was looking for. She pointed at the front page and stepped back so Serenity could see. A young boy, who could have only been a year older than Travis had been, was pictured. A long line of stitches ran from his hairline, over his eyebrow, missing his eye and restarting on his cheek, ending at his chin. The caption said he had over one hundred and fifty stitches in the one wound. He had over a thousand stitches on various wounds all over his body.

Serenity devoured the article. The boy's story mirrored her own. He was wandering the deepest part of the forest along the bayou, crying out and begging for help. When some hikers found him, he collapsed and screamed about Willie taking his sister. The police interviewed him, but he never mentioned a boat. He only spoke about the monster who took his sister. The police labeled him, just like they had her, a disturbed child who was making up stories to help cope with the loss.

"This was only two years ago. Where is this boy now?" Serenity asked.

Evelyn flipped through the papers again and when she stopped, Serenity noted she had skipped to a year after the story about the girl disappearing. This time, Evelyn stopped on the obituary page. A picture of the boy, before the scarring to his face, smiled from the page. There was a brief paragraph speaking about the boy, his birth, his parents, his sister and who he left behind in death. The last line caused Serenity's eyes to fill with tears. It read, "He and his sister are together once again."

"He committed suicide. They don't say that here, but I remember when the news of his death got out. He couldn't handle the nightmares, couldn't handle what happened to his sister. He took two bottles of prescription medication and let himself drown in the bathtub."

Serenity swiped at the tears that wet her cheeks. There had been so many times she had felt the same way. She couldn't fault the boy. When no one believed her. When she struggled with the nightmares of Travis, the steamboat and Willie, they just prescribed medications. Leaving home and starting over in Savannah, meeting Daphne, was what had saved her life.

Weight of Knowledge

FOR THE REST OF the morning, Evelyn helped Serenity track down the stories of mysterious disappearances on the bayou. Some of them seemed too far-fetched to be what she was looking for. Evelyn was more than happy to discuss each story she had researched. She helped Serenity disregard the ones that were proven to be something other than supernatural, and soon, Serenity had pages of notes on stories that seemed similar to her own nightmare.

Her stomach growling was the signal Serenity had been in the library for far too long. She looked at her watch and realized she had missed lunch, and it was almost dinnertime. Looking over at Evelyn, she studied the woman. Not for the first time. Likely older than her own mother, the woman was definitely obsessed with the steamboat and Willie.

"Why did you become interested in this?" Serenity asked, trying to sound as nonchalant as possible.

Evelyn's head snapped up, and she looked at Serenity quickly. The way she looked only made Serenity more suspicious of this overly helpful woman. But as if she could read Serenity's thoughts, Evelyn's face relaxed and her normal, soft smile appeared.

"Oh, well, I guess I just got curious. And as I looked into things, it became clear there was something going on. What I haven't been able to figure out is if someone is covering this all up, or it's just so impossible for people to truly believe."

The explanation sounded plausible enough. But Serenity still felt something was off. She was thankful for the help Evelyn had provided, but she was ready to grab dinner and head back to her hotel. There was so much information now, and she was feeling overwhelmed by it. Adding the strange woman, who seemed to appear out of nowhere and just at the right time, was too much for her mind to handle.

"Well, thank you for your help. I'm going to go now. This has given me a lot to think about." Serenity packed the films back into the box the librarian had brought them in.

"What do you plan to do?"

Serenity just shrugged, not sure if she was ready to tell Evelyn the truth. She had been light on details of what had brought her back home, but the woman had asked multiple times, prying into her life. She tried to ask about Serenity's parents and what she had been doing the last few years, but each question went unanswered. The part that made Serenity most nervous was the fact that Evelyn knew the anniversary of Travis's disappearance was coming.

"Go back to my hotel?" Serenity answered, though she knew Evelyn didn't mean that.

Evelyn's eyes narrowed, but she pressed her mouth into a small smile, the corners of her mouth tight with annoyance. "Of course, dear. Have a wonderful night."

Serenity hefted the box of film into her arms and hurried from the room. A different librarian was at the front desk, but she smiled warmly when Serenity returned the films. Outside, the sun was getting low in the sky, but the summer warmth had not died off. Although the humidity was thick, Serenity wasn't bothered. Humidity was a fact of life for her.

She glanced over her shoulder more than once as she rushed down the street toward a corner deli. Evelyn was nowhere in sight, but Serenity didn't relax until she was in her hotel room with dinner and a bottle of wine. She changed into lounge clothes and ate her dinner faster than necessary.

As she sipped her wine, she watched the moon outside her window. She tried to figure out what it was about Evelyn that bothered her. It would be unfair to say she hadn't been an immense help. Serenity wouldn't have found half of the stories she did without the woman's aid, but Evelyn's excitement bothered her whenever her story was mentioned.

In the end, she didn't find one other story that referenced the steamboat. Only the one that talked about Willie. And sadly, as the boy had taken his own life, there was no one she could talk to about that. Some stories could have been considered similar to her own, but none offered any clues about how or where to find the steamboat.

Swirling the wine in her glass, she tried not to think about how it was the color of blood. She thought about Travis. Was it his soul calling out for her? And the dreams she was having. Were they similar to what the boy had before he killed himself? Was it the feeling that he'd failed his sister, combined with the fact that he couldn't stop dreaming about it, that made him leave this world? There were so many unanswered questions. Serenity knew she would never have all the answers.

As she got ready for bed, she played a meditation, to help her mind quiet. Nothing ever worked for her one hundred percent of the time, but she didn't stop trying to get a quiet night's sleep. When she slid under the sheets, she continued to do her breathing exercises as the meditation turned into white noise, meant to help her fall asleep. And for once, all of her work paid off. She slept through the night without dreaming about anything at all.

The next day, she stayed in her hotel room and plotted out the times and rough locations from the stories she had found at the library. With a topographical map of the bayou, she used small flag Post-its to mark each place she thought could be the likely location of disappearances. She had fourteen likely Willie incidents, with another nine that she wasn't positive about.

In the end, when she leaned back and looked at the map, she felt a shiver run up her spine. She had a special color arrow for Travis, and she marked the place she knew they had seen the Steamboat. It was a location she would never forget. The rest of the arrows circled the same bend in the river, creating almost a spiral of the area.

Now she knew the where. What she couldn't be sure about was the when. And she had to decide what to do when she found him.

The Fog of Deception

Serenity's phone rang, startling her from studying the map. Picking it up, she checked the screen and was glad to see Daphne's name.

"Hi, Daph."

"Girl, you've been gone almost two days and not a call or a text?"

Serenity grimaced. With everything going on, she had been wrapped up in her own head and had forgotten to let Daphne know she was okay. "I'm sorry. Things have been complicated since I got back."

"Your parents?"

"They kicked me out."

Daphne's gasp was audible across the call. "They did what? Those bastards!"

"Apparently Mama's quilting club is more important than her daughter. At least that's the gist of it." Serenity leaned back and rubbed her eyes. Her parents' disregard stung. She couldn't pretend it didn't.

"Are you going to come home?"

"Not yet. I...I'm not sure what I need to do. But I know I'm not done." Serenity took a deep breath and told Daphne about the increase in the nightmares. Then she went through what she had found at the library, Evelyn, and the map she was currently looking at.

"This is heavy, Itty," Daphne said after a really long pause.

"I know, I'm sorry."

"What are you sorry for? You didn't kick yourself out. You didn't ask for this to happen to you when you were a kid. And you don't want to have these nightmares. There's nothing to say sorry for."

Serenity wanted to cry again, but this time, it was in thankfulness. Without the support of Daphne over the last couple of years, she probably would have ended up just like the teen boy she'd read about.

"So, this woman you met. Do you think she could be helpful?" Daphne continued while Serenity reined in her emotions.

"She was pretty helpful with the newspapers. A little too helpful. It was as if she just knew I would be there, or someone would be there looking into this. It felt too coincidental."

Daphne made an agreeing noise. "I can see that. Just keep your eyes open. If you're not coming home, does that mean you're going to be on the river?"

The idea of being on the river, especially alone, chilled Serenity to her bones. But she wasn't sure what other options she had. "I think so."

"I could come help you."

Serenity felt a slam of panic at the idea. "No, Daph. Absolutely not. I'm not putting anyone else in danger."

"Just yourself?"

"I'm the only one who can do this. It's me Travis is calling."

Daphne sighed. "Itty, I understand that with your shitty parents, you feel little self-worth. It makes me want to drive over there, just to punch one of them in the mouth. You are worth saving. You are worth this life. You can't sacrifice yourself for Travis. He's gone. You would be sacrificing yourself for a ghost."

"I don't plan on becoming a human sacrifice. Don't worry."

"I'll keep worrying until your butt is back home, where it belongs."

They chatted about a workplace drama Daphne was going through and said their goodbyes. The conversation with her friend helped wipe some cobwebs from her mind. She had again missed meals and was ravenous. The research was pushing her to a breaking point, and she knew she needed her strength if she was going to do anything about Willie.

She powered up her laptop and ordered food to her door, thankful for the world of technology. Not that she was afraid to leave her room. She just wanted to be alone a little while longer. An emotion tugged inside her, making her feel like something was going to end and she wanted the chance to be ready for it.

While she waited, she searched for any sort of store that dealt with the occult. The results of the search surprised her. She had never realized how many stores there were in the general area that dealt with witchcraft, magic, myths, and legends. There were reviews on some of them, which Serenity read. She found ones that seemed to know what they were talking about and wrote down the addresses.

Her food arrived, and she distracted herself with a sitcom on cable TV. She decided on a plan of action. In the morning, she planned to visit the highest-rated occult shop first. There was also a new age store she thought could be useful. In her research, she couldn't decide if Willie was a monster made of flesh and bone, or something metaphysical that she didn't understand. She was cautiously optimistic, hoping someone at one of the shops could guide her in the right direction.

She had not even finished her meditation when sleep overcame her. Before she realized it, her body felt like it was bobbing and rolling. Blinking, she opened her eyes to find herself in the middle of the river, sitting in a decaying rowboat. She tried to steady herself by holding onto the sides of the boat. There were no oars to row herself anywhere, the boat just moved with the water.

"Serenity!" A voice pierced the silence, a voice she knew.

Though she knew she was on the river, she was surrounded by dense fog. There were no visible markers around her to tell her where on the river she was. The stillness and silence were unnatural, as if the entire bayou was frozen, waiting to take a breath.

"Travis!" Her scream seemed to echo.

Her heart pounded as she swung her head from side to side, trying to find even a glimpse of her friend.

"Ser! I'm over here!" Travis's voice came from beyond the suffocating fog, impossible to pinpoint, but Serenity continued to look.

The boat creaked under her as she leaned forward, urging the vessel to move faster. She had no way of controlling the speed, but she hoped she was headed in the right direction for Travis. If she could see any hint of a location, she could have a place to start her search.

"Where are you?" she yelled back, her voice vibrating with urgency.

"Here, I'm here, Ser!"

With each echoed word, Serenity had the impression Travis was right around the corner. It felt as if she could reach out and touch him with her fingertips through the fog. But when she let go of the side of the boat and stretched her arm out, it only disappeared in the fog, touching nothing solid.

"You're almost there." Travis's words were quieter now, as if he was whispering near her shoulder.

Serenity spun as far as she could in the boat without throwing herself overboard, but there was no one there. She straightened herself, causing the boat to tilt dangerously, before it calmed and continued its slow bob down the water. The sky above her was darkening, the fog becoming a deeper gray. That was her only signal that there was no sun.

Abruptly, her boat stopped moving, and it was only her grip on the sides that kept her from pitching forward. A rumble began through the fog, and Serenity strained to hear and determine what was making the noise. After a moment, the rumble changed, and she could hear a demonic laugh through the deep sound. The hair on her arms stood to attention, and she trembled.

"You'll never reach him," a voice sneered, taunting her. Willie.

His laughter began again, just as the fog in front of her parted, revealing the steamboat, half sunk, just as she remembered it. On the main deck, she could see Travis in the shadows, his hand reaching out toward her.

"I'm coming, Travis! Just hold on! I'm coming!" Serenity cried.

Willie's laughter reverberated around her. "Come this way, Serenity. Come join us. Everything you seek is inside."

In front of her eyes, Willie materialized behind Travis.

"Serenity! Please!" Travis's voice was clearer now, filled with urgency and panic.

The grotesque shell of the steamboat loomed above as her small boat collided with the side. She reached up toward where she last saw Travis, but her hand touched nothing but air. With fear tightening its grip around her chest, Serenity grabbed onto the side of the steamboat. Finding handholds, she carefully pulled herself up until she could put her feet on the main deck.

Travis was gone, taken by Willie to whatever sunken prison he kept him in. Serenity slowly made her way along the main deck, remembering the time she and Travis thought exploring the boat would be a fun afternoon. The rotten wood beneath her feet creaked and bowed, feeling as if it would give way at any moment.

"Join us…" Willie's mangled words came from deep inside the steamboat, a place Serenity couldn't see.

"Travis! Don't listen to him! Follow my voice!"

Willie cackled, and Travis cried out in pain. The sound cut deep into Serenity's mind and she cried out, lurching toward the place she knew she had fallen into the belly of the steamboat. But as she tried to get to the hole, it continued to move further away, taking Willie's laugh with it.

Suddenly, Serenity was flung backward. As her body flipped head over feet, she could see the black of the bayou rising to meet her. Splashing into the water, she felt herself sink, no longer able to fight the pull of the darkness inside her.

The Witching Willow

SERENITY AWOKE IN A cold sweat, gasping for breath. Her room was just lightening with the morning sun. But in her mind, she was still drowning in her nightmare, her sorrow, and her fear. Staring at the white textured ceiling, she worked to ground herself and clarify that she was safe in her hotel room.

She shivered through her shower, even with the water as hot as she could manage. Her mind couldn't let go of the sound of Willie's laughter. She had never heard it in real life, couldn't remember hearing it the day he took Travis. Now, her mind was filling in horrors she had never actually experienced. However, it only made her more certain that it was Travis sending her the dreams.

Pulling herself together, she dressed and tied her wet hair into a bun on top of her head. With her purse on her shoulder, she grabbed the list of stores and headed out the door. She wasn't sure what she would need, or if it was magic, that could get rid of Willie. But she hoped someone in one shop could lead her in the right direction.

The first shop was a bust. A teenage girl stood behind the counter and barely looked up at Serenity as she asked about specific products. Her thumb never stopped swiping on the screen of her phone, even as she shrugged to show she didn't know the answer to the question she was being asked. Serenity had sighed and quietly left the shop. She wondered what it was like to be a typical teenager without the weight of the world on your shoulders.

The next shop was no longer in business. Instead, it was a small boutique clothing reseller. Serenity didn't even bother to look inside, figuring they weren't hiding any occult supplies in a back storeroom. In her rental car, she marked off the two top choices. Shaking her head, she mentally thought of all the ways she could torture the department of people that were responsible for keeping listings up to date on a search engine.

The third shop wasn't in town. From the map, Serenity had her doubts about it actually being at the address listed. But she put her car in gear, turned up her music and followed the GPS directions. As she drove down a tree-lined highway, she let some of her worries slip away and enjoyed the sunny morning.

The GPS warned her that her turn was coming, and she slowly took her foot from the gas. Searching, she didn't see the turn until she had almost missed it. Slamming on her brakes, she took the tight right-hand turn down a gravel road. Tree branches intertwined overhead, casting the world in shadow. Serenity kept her eyes on the road, afraid her mind would play tricks on her if she were to look into the dark forest on either side.

Her rental bumped along the pitted road as she continued to follow the gravel road for another mile. At a dead end sat a small cabin. Under a cover of moss and vines, Serenity could make out a wrap-around porch. Lines of chimes hung on each side of the door. The wind pushed them around and she could hear their music from inside her car.

Parking, she studied the building, wondering if the address she found was incorrect. She hesitated until the screen door opened and a young woman stepped out. Holding a hand up to shield her eyes, she faced Serenity's car. Serenity could feel her gaze and knew she must look strange just sitting in front of the cabin, not getting out of her vehicle.

With a deep breath and plastering on a smile, Serenity popped open the door and climbed out. Holding her hand up in greeting, she faced the woman. "Hi. I'm sorry, I might be in the wrong place. I'm looking for the Witching Willow?"

"You found it. This is my shop. Come on in." The woman turned and entered the cabin, leaving the screen door propped open.

Inside, Serenity was instantly sure this was the right place to find what she needed. She slowly circled the large interior of the cabin. One wall held drying herbs hanging in bundles along the shelves or already in labeled jars. There were shelves of glass bowls, full of different colored crystals. She ran her fingers along a very large individual crystal that sat between bowls. Candles of all shapes and colors lined another set of shelves.

"Can I help you find something?" The woman behind the counter couldn't have been much older than Serenity. She wore a flowing dress with a deep-colored floral pattern and several chains around her neck, each bearing a different amulet. Her kind smile put Serenity at ease, settling the butterflies in her stomach.

"I'm not sure what I'm looking for, if I'm being honest."

The woman tilted her head to the side, pulling her bottom lip between her teeth as she studied Serenity.

"Protection, I think."

Serenity rubbed her sweaty hands on her jean shorts. Her eyes darted around the cabin, wondering how the woman had read her so well.

"It's a gift, but your aura screams fear," the woman said, reading Serenity's thoughts.

"It does?"

The woman nodded her head, but they were interrupted when the cabin door opened again. Both women looked over at the sound of the tinkling doorbell. Serenity went cold when she realized she knew the person who walked through.

"Serenity, what a coincidence!" Evelyn's voice was high-pitched and grated on Serenity's anxiety.

The Witching Willow was off the beaten path, and Serenity had never told the woman what her next steps were. She was immediately wary of her as she walked into the shop. The woman behind the counter looked between the two of them curiously. Serenity eyed the door. She didn't want to leave, because it was the first shop she had found that could have what she needed. But Evelyn appearing made her nervous.

Seeming to pick up on the tension, the woman walked out from behind her counter. "Hi. Can I help you?"

Evelyn looked over at the woman, as if she hadn't even realized she was there until that moment. A dark look seemed to cross her face before her mouth stretched into a large smile. She gestured around the shop. "Oh, I'm sure I can find what I need."

The shop owner smiled, but it was clear she wasn't buying anything Evelyn was dishing out. "I'm the owner of this shop. I can help you find what you need much faster. Let me guess, a few candles?"

"Oh, I have plenty of candles at home," Evelyn replied with a fake laugh.

Serenity watched the two of them, still glancing at the door every now and then, as if she could bolt and get away from the older woman. But before she could run, the shop owner turned to her, completely ignoring Evelyn. "We were just stepping into the back, weren't we, Serenity?"

Relief flooded her, and Serenity nodded. Without a look at Evelyn, the shop owner motioned for Serenity to follow her and made her way toward a door at the far end of the shop. When she opened it, Serenity stood in a colorful living room.

The door shut behind them, and the shop owner moved toward a galley kitchen at the far end of the room. "Your fear got so much louder when that woman walked in. Is it her you need protection from?"

Gazing at the closed door, imagining Evelyn listening on the other side, Serenity just shook her head. But the shop owner wasn't looking at her. While Serenity stood frozen in her spot, not sure where to move, the shop owner busied herself filling a teapot and turning on the stove.

"My name is Ember. I'm sorry for reading you earlier. I try not to read people without asking, but I couldn't seem to help myself."

"How does that work?"

Ember shrugged. "It's just something I've always been able to do. Sometimes it's colors. I see them, glowing, or moving around a person. And sometimes, I just hear things."

"You said my aura was screaming in fear. And got louder when Evelyn walked in." Serenity wandered toward a bookcase, afraid to look the woman in the eye.

"I think your aura knows something you don't."

A Safe Space

EMBER LEFT SERENITY TO sip fragrant herbal tea, while she went back out to the shop. The Wiccan shop owner seemed to know exactly what needed to happen. She made Serenity comfortable at her small dining table and promised to be right back. When she opened the shop door, she greeted Evelyn with a loud, bright voice and closed the door firmly behind her.

That gave Serenity the chance to look around the cabin living area. The space felt less occult and more comfortable living. There was a big brown couch that was covered in crocheted afghan blankets. The kitchen cabinets had no doors, revealing mismatched plates, bowls, and an overabundance of mugs. Paintings of various things, some that Serenity couldn't even begin to guess, were hung all over the walls. None of the decor had any plan or matched. But it put Serenity at ease.

The tea was almost gone when the door to the shop opened again. Ember breezed in without a care in the world. When she didn't close the door, Serenity leaned so she could see through it and the shop looked empty.

"She's gone. Took some time to convince her you were completing a crystal cleansing in my private space. Not that a cleansing would be a bad idea for you, but we can discuss that later." She moved to the stove, turning the burner on under the teapot again. "That woman has secrets. I assume you think she followed you here?"

"I'm not really sure what to think."

Ember turned with raised eyebrows. "Your words don't match what I can see hanging around you. I'm not sure what brought you to my door, Serenity. But if feels like the universe put you in my path for a reason."

Serenity sighed, wondering why everything she was feeling suddenly wanted to bubble to the surface and explode from her mouth. Before she could speak, Ember had refilled her tea and placed new tea leaves in the strainer. The woman sat across from Serenity with her own mug, and she watched her as she slowly dunked the strainer into her hot water.

"She must have followed me. Your shop is so out of the way. And it's the third place I tried today. She also didn't know I was going to be checking out occult shops," Serenity explained.

"But she does know you. And knows the reason you're visiting my shop." Ember's words weren't a question, but a statement of fact that she seemed to have gleaned from everything that had transpired in the shop.

"Yes. Well, she doesn't really know me. We only spent some time together in the library a few days ago."

Ember nodded. "I see."

"She recognized me, or at least claimed to. From the news. I guess you might not know about who I am and what happened a few years ago."

"Oh, I know who you are. But it wasn't my place to blurt out that you are the girl that survived and had a wild story that no one would believe." Ember leaned forward slightly, locking her gaze with Serenity's. "Except me. I always believed it."

"Does everyone remember who I am?" Serenity whispered into her teacup.

Ember smiled brightly and leaned back in her chair. "Not everyone, I'm sure. But those of us that are interested or educated in the occult couldn't help but follow your story."

"Why?"

"Because a lot of us are curious about the supernatural. And what happened to you couldn't have been of this world."

Serenity was surprised by Ember's ease in speaking about what had happened to her. For years, she had been used to being disregarded, argued with, and looked down upon. Daphne had been the only one in her life to believe her and not make her feel crazy. She felt at a loss for words.

Ember seemed to understand, and she tittered. "Not used to that, are you? I saw what they said about you in the news. As a teenager, I can imagine that was difficult to hear."

"It wasn't a simple time."

"But you're back. There must be a reason for that."

Serenity didn't speak, just nodded and sipped tea.

"And I can feel that it has something to do with that day, with what happened to you."

Ember didn't wait for Serenity to answer. She stood and went to a chest of drawers against one wall. Whispering to herself, she sorted through items, pushing one drawer in before pulling another out. She made a small noise of exclamation as she closed the last drawer and came back to the table. She set down a small velvet pouch before sitting across from Serenity again.

Opening the pouch, Ember turned it upside down, allowing three crystals to tumble out onto the table. The first Serenity picked up was a small tower, black, with gray swirls through the opaque color. Another, she recognized as obsidian, its surface shiny and smooth, reflective almost like glass. The last was a mixture of light lavender and deep purple. It was rough and oddly shaped, with jagged formations.

"Black tourmaline, obsidian, and amethyst. Together, these crystals are powerful protectors against negative energies. You should keep these on you at all times. I can't begin to understand what you are here to face. But we can work on making sure you're prepared," Ember said.

Serenity put the crystals back into the small pouch and cinched it. "I'm not sure three small rocks are going to help."

"Maybe if you tell me what it is you are trying to do, I will have a better idea," Ember prompted.

With a deep breath, Serenity spat out, "I'm here to find the steamboat and free my friend's soul from the clutches of Steamboat Willie, destroying the monster at the same time, if I can."

Ember's eyes widened, and she looked at the small pouch. "You're right. Those rocks will not do the job by themselves."

By lunchtime, with Ember closing the shop for the day, they had collected several items that Serenity could use for protection. She wasn't positive she believed in any of it. However, Ember believed her story, and she believed in Willie. And that pushed Serenity into trusting the shopkeeper. As they sorted through supplies and Ember researched additional resources, Serenity told her bits and pieces about her dreams and what had happened to Travis. The woman listened with compassion and disputed none of her story.

Ember insisted on doing a smudging on Serenity. Lighting a bundle of herbs that Serenity couldn't name, the woman walked around her, allowing the smoke to flow around her body. She didn't speak as she blew on the bundle, causing more smoke to cleanse Serenity. The light music that played on the shop speakers was enough to relax Serenity as she stood still, allowing Ember to move around her freely.

"I would feel better if you took a few bundles with you. You could light them in whatever boat you use on the bayou and maybe keep yourself cleansed until the last moment."

"I don't think I could do that alone."

Ember finished the smudging, setting the smoldering bundle in a glass dish on the counter. "I could go with you."

Serenity didn't even need to think about it. She couldn't put anyone else at risk. "Absolutely not."

Their eyes met. Serenity held Ember's gaze without blinking, hoping she could convey how serious she was. Ember smiled softly and shrugged her shoulders, before going back to the bundles of herbs she had on a shelf. Over her shoulder she spoke, "I'm not really itching to face down whatever type of demon this Willie is, so I'll respect whatever you decide. Just seems like you shouldn't be shouldering this burden on your own."

"It's been my burden all along."

Secrets and Lies

EMBER WALKED SERENITY TO her car, both of them looking around at the trees that surrounded the cabin. Though they said nothing, it was clear neither of them was sure Evelyn had gone far. The only sound, other than their footsteps, was the breeze through the trees.

At the rental car, Ember loaded a bag with the products she had chosen for Serenity. She turned and took a deep breath. "I'm going to just repeat that I don't believe you should go about this on your own. You survived once, and you were lucky."

"I only survived because Travis sacrificed himself."

"He wouldn't want that sacrifice to be for nothing."

Serenity looked away, Ember's gaze feeling too deep, as if she could dig into her soul. "I can't give up."

Serenity's eyes snapped back to Ember's when the woman took her hands. Her palms were warm, and she squeezed Serenity's hands. "I understand where you're at, Serenity. I realize that just because I can see your aura, feel your fear and sadness, I still cannot understand what you're going through. But what I do know is, this will be the most dangerous thing you will ever do in your life."

Carefully, Serenity pulled her hands away. She gave Ember a sad smile. "I know. I've lived with the nightmares of what is out there. I know what I may be facing."

Ember nodded. The women said their goodbyes and moments later, Serenity was bumping down the gravel road in her rental car. Her mind raced with all the information Ember had given her. The Wiccan had been a better supply of details than the library had. Between Ember and her network of witches, she could confirm that Serenity and the boy that had committed suicide were the only two survivors to talk about the monster.

However, the two stories were all the local Wiccans needed to believe there was something in the bayou. Ember told stories of the feelings of power that came from the river and its surroundings, and how many witches had drawn strength from it. But she also mentioned that she knew of at least one practicing witch who had left because the power had driven her mad. The woman couldn't handle being in the area any longer and last Ember had heard, she was living a quiet life in the middle of the country.

Serenity didn't have time to track down any additional witches, and there was nothing more they could provide. And she would not allow Ember anywhere near the steamboat. There was a natural curiosity the witch had about something truly supernatural that she could see and touch. But it wasn't a game. The danger outweighed everything else.

Back at her hotel, Serenity took out the items that Ember had packed for her. She had the pouch of crystals to keep on her. There was a bag full of bundled herbs, the same as she used during the smudging session. She wasn't sure the actual cleansing had done any good, but Ember had looked at her and nodded her head as if her aura, or whatever she saw around Serenity, looked better. There were two colored candles, each for a specific purpose. And a large bag of salt.

In the bag's bottom, there was another pouch, one that Serenity didn't remember Ember giving her. Carefully, she opened it and poured the two items and a slip of paper into her palm. One of the items was a small jar, filled with herbs, a nail, salt and a piece of paper. A cork sealed the jar, and wax covered it. The other item was a long gold chain with a pendant at the end. The pendant, shaped like a sun, had an eye in the center, with a dark green stone for a pupil.

Serenity opened the piece of paper and read the quick note Ember had scrawled for her.

Though you refuse to take my help in person, I wanted to help with your nightmares. Put the jar under your mattress and wear the pendant at all times. Both will ward off evil and more. Good luck. – E

Without hesitation, Serenity slipped the gold chain over her head. She picked up the small bottle and shook it, listening to the small items tinkling inside. She shrugged, admitting that trying to understand the rules of the occult was not on her agenda. Carefully, she slipped the small bottle under the side of the mattress where she slept. She couldn't contain the hope that bloomed at the thought of a decent night's sleep—one without her dead best friend in her dreams.

A knock at her door startled her, and she froze, wondering who it could be.

"Serenity? I know this is your room and your rental car was in the parking lot," a voice called through the door.

The hope that Serenity had been feeling popped like a balloon in her chest. She knew the voice. But she couldn't be sure how she had been found again. Serenity's hope vanished, replaced by anger. She was finished being anyone's victim. Stalking to the door, she ripped it open with such force that it slipped from her fingers and slammed into the wall. Evelyn jumped, her eyes wide as she took in Serenity.

"Umm, sorry, am I interrupting something?"

"You mean like at the Witching Willow? Or how about the library? Because I don't believe that was a coincidence, either." Serenity's voice was stone, much stronger than she was actually feeling.

Evelyn had the audacity to not look guilty as she shrugged. "I followed you."

"Obviously. What do you want, Evelyn?"

"Can I come in? This probably isn't a conversation for a hallway where just anyone can hear."

Serenity looked out into the hall and didn't see anyone. She looked back at Evelyn, not willing to just let her into the hotel room.

"Now, Serenity, do you want even more people to think you're crazy?"

"That isn't the leverage you think it is. What these people think of me no longer matters to me."

Evelyn raised an eyebrow at her, a challenge in her eyes. "I know when to find the Steamboat."

Serenity froze, staring at the woman. "If that were true, you would have said something before."

"If I had just blurted that out at the library, would you have believed me?"

Serenity didn't have to say anything. The answer was obvious. There would have been no reason to think Evelyn was anything more than a loon that had latched onto her survival story.

"What do you want?" Serenity repeated her question. She didn't believe Evelyn was just offering to tell her something so important for free.

"I want to go with you when you go to find it."

Serenity's mind turned over the request. She wouldn't put Ember in danger, because the Wiccan was kind and pure, but Evelyn meant nothing to her. Nevertheless, she was someone that felt like a threat, even if Serenity couldn't put a finger on what the threat truly was.

"No."

Evelyn crossed her arms and leaned against the doorjamb in a relaxed manner. "Then I won't be giving you the information I have."

"No one has found the steamboat in years. It doesn't just appear in a specific place and time. I highly doubt you, of all people, could find it."

And Serenity meant that. Evelyn was an older woman, who couldn't have been searching the bayou on her own. She would have been easy prey for Willie if she had found the steamboat. Her gray hair, now that it wasn't pulled into a bun, formed a wild halo around her head and made her look older. There was no way she would be a help in finding the boat, Willie or Travis.

"I know how to predict where and when it will appear."

Serenity tried to scrutinize her words. There was no way she would just believe Evelyn was telling the absolute truth. But she wasn't sure if she could pass up the chance at knowing how to find the boat. She felt like she was walking a fine line and was worried that if she let Evelyn into her room, into her search, into her life, she would doom herself.

"Coming to my hotel room, uninvited, or following me at all, isn't the way to help me. I'm tired. We can meet in the morning." Pushing back the meeting for at least a few hours gave Serenity the chance to be on equal footing with the older woman.

"Breakfast. The café on the corner. 9 a.m."

With that, Evelyn walked down the hall, toward the stairs. Serenity didn't close the door until she saw her disappear through the door of the stairs. When she closed the door, she was sure to flip the deadbolt. Even then, she still looked through the peephole to make sure Evelyn wasn't lurking around the corridor.

Serenity had a bad feeling about letting Evelyn into the search for the steamboat. But she felt like if she could handle the woman in front of her, it would be better than being followed everywhere she went.

The Numbers Align

BREAKFAST CAME EARLY, BUT Serenity was thankful to have gotten a restful night's sleep. Her hand came up, so she could run her fingers around the sun amulet. She couldn't be sure that she slept nightmare-free because of the necklace and jar from Ember. But Travis and Willie were nowhere to be found in her dreams.

Serenity got to the café early, so Evelyn couldn't surprise her yet again. She ordered a coffee and a muffin before taking a small corner table in the back of the café. From her vantage point, she could clearly see the front door and wait for Evelyn.

The older woman arrived exactly on time and, as she removed her sunglasses, her eyes found Serenity almost immediately. A smile crossed her face, but it wasn't a friendly one, and Serenity felt a chill go through her. Evelyn took her time, waiting in line at the counter to order her breakfast. She smiled and talked sweetly to the employee behind the counter. All the while Serenity watched her, trying to figure it all out.

When she finally sat down across from Serenity, her sweet old lady persona was in place, and she settled back in the chair.

"You showed up," she said.

"If I hadn't, you would have just kept following me."

Evelyn's smile widened a fraction, as if she was happy Serenity was catching on. "Most likely."

"If you know how to find the steamboat, why do you need me? Why do you want to find it in the first place?"

"General curiosity."

Serenity let out a humorless laugh. "I don't believe that for a second."

"My reasons are my own. But we both have the same goal, I think." Evelyn watched Serenity over her coffee cup as she sipped.

"My goals are none of your business. I came here on my own, alone, for a reason."

"You're looking for the steamboat. I want to find it too. Our reasons for that are different, but the goals are the same."

"If you can't be honest about why you want to find a supernatural steamboat that houses an evil demon, then this conversation is over." Serenity decided to just throw it all out in the open. Evelyn was aware of the stories she had told the police after Travis went missing. There was no reason for her to deny that now.

Evelyn seemed to contemplate Serenity's terms. She crossed her arms over her chest and shook her head. Muttering to herself, she sighed and stared at Serenity. The old lady smile was gone, anger now burning in her eyes.

"I've been obsessed with the supernatural for most of my adult life. In this podunk area of the country, most things you hear about are cryptids that are never proven. Now, with everyone having high-definition cameras in their pockets, there should be more proof. But your story. It was different. You came out of the bayou, terrified and injured. Something got to you out there. And that same something took your friend. So, I followed your story. But you left town as soon as you could and didn't come back until now. When I heard a rumor that you had returned to your childhood home and your parents had turned you away, I knew I needed to find you."

Serenity sat in shock. She didn't know anyone even realized she had come home, let alone that her parents had kicked her out. She didn't even tell Daphne until she was in the hotel and had already met Evelyn. Her eyes scanned the room, looking for anyone that was paying too much attention to her. Evelyn seemed to pick up on what she was doing.

"It's less likely in this town for anyone to realize who you are. But when you went back to your tiny hometown, well, that was news that spread like wildfire through the few that still live there. I have kept connections in that area, just for this exact reason."

"To find me?" Serenity asked in a small voice.

"Well, the only other survivor of Willie couldn't handle what came with that. I only talked to him once, but it was clear the nightmares and memories were going to swallow him."

"And you just watched that happen, I guess."

Evelyn's hard face softened for a moment and some sort of emotion that Serenity couldn't name crossed her eyes. But then she set her mouth in a hard line and all sense of a real person was gone. "He wasn't my responsibility. There was nothing I could do for him."

"Did you even want to help him?" Serenity meant to ask the question in her own head, but it popped out of her mouth.

Evelyn's face darkened, and she leaned forward, as if she was going to climb across the table. "I don't know what you are implying, Serenity. But I don't think I like it."

When the woman had walked into the small room in the library, she had struck Serenity as a lonely old lady, just looking for someone to talk to. Her knowledge of Serenity's story had struck her as odd and coincidental. However, Serenity had given her the benefit of the doubt and ignored the weird feeling that was rolling in her gut.

Now, it was clear that this was the real Evelyn. She had been stalking Serenity since she returned to town. Obsession over Willie and the steamboat had pushed her to the point of bending the law to get what she wanted. The piece that seemed to still be missing for Serenity was why she had the obsession in the first place.

"I'm not implying anything," Serenity mumbled into her coffee mug. She had no one nearby that could help her deal with Evelyn. She was completely alone. Angering the woman didn't seem like the right move.

Evelyn leaned back in her chair again, tapping a nail on her coffee mug rim. Without another word, she reached into her large purse and pulled out a square of paper. She pushed it across the table to Serenity. Unfolding it, Serenity found it wasn't just one page, but three. There were star charts, water level measurements, and current charts.

Looking at Evelyn, Serenity just waited for the explanation.

"It's the numbers. The current and water level have to be a specific measurement, and the planet has to be on a specific rotation. When those three line up, the boat appears," Evelyn explained. She looked at Serenity as if that explained everything.

"Travis and I weren't out at night," Serenity replied.

Evelyn rolled her eyes. "Dear girl, even if you can't see them, there are stars in the sky."

Serenity knew that. She wasn't a complete idiot, even if that was how Evelyn was looking at her. She went back to studying the pages, her face heating.

"So, what's the point?" Serenity asked.

"All of those numbers. They line up in two days."

Serenity felt the room shift and spin. Gripping the table with both hands, she let the pages fall to the floor. She couldn't stop the tumble of her stomach as the words Evelyn spoke settled in her mind. Two days. The numbers lined up in two days. The anniversary of Travis's disappearance and the day Serenity survived Steamboat Willie.

Whispers in the Fog

It took a long moment for Serenity's vision to clear and for her to stop feeling like she would pass out. Evelyn stooped and picked up the pages and smoothed them out on the table. Then she waited, watching Serenity, as if she was about to unlock the secrets of the universe for her.

But when the silence stretched between them, Evelyn sighed and leaned forward on the table again. "These numbers line up perfectly every few years. As I'm sure you can guess, the measurements two years ago, when the other survivor was on the steamboat, were the exact same as the day you also found the steamboat over six years ago."

When Serenity didn't respond, Evelyn continued. "It's all connected. Don't you see, Serenity? You came back just in time, for a reason. The nightmares have probably called to you. Because you escaped. You're the only one that he hasn't been able to keep. And now you're back. Looking for the steamboat."

"What's the point?!" Serenity finally found her voice, and it was louder than she had expected, drawing a few looks from neighboring tables.

Evelyn ignored the surrounding people, and a sinister smile appeared on her face. "The point is, he wants you. So he'll appear. For you."

Serenity's hands tightened on the table, her knuckles going white. She wasn't sure she could let go. The table felt like the only real thing at the moment, the only thing keeping her from sprinting from the café and never looking back. Not that she understood why she had been drawn back to her home. She didn't truly know what the nightmares were saying, but her heart told her she needed to free Travis—no matter how, it just needed to happen. Somewhere in her subconscious, she knew it could lead to her own death. However, she had never imagined Willie wanted her specifically.

"Don't be naïve, Serenity. What did you think was happening?" Evelyn asked.

"I...I don't know," Serenity whispered.

Evelyn casually finished her coffee and popped the last bit of her muffin into her mouth. She watched Serenity the whole time. Slowly, Serenity urged each of her fingers to release the table. She pulled her arms in, wrapping them around her middle, trying to figure out her next step.

"So, we'll meet in two days. You know where. The same place you and Travis launched your boat that day. I have a boat that will get us there. If you want the nightmares to stop, you'll be there."

Evelyn didn't wait for her response. She stood and walked toward the café door, without a backward glance. Serenity sat frozen in her spot. Each of her muscles was tense, and she fought her internal urge to run. She felt so alone. There was no one to save her, no one to turn to that could provide comfort.

People came and went into the café until the lunch rush. A café worker approached Serenity and asked her if she needed anything else. That was what finally shook Serenity out of her terrified state. Embarrassed, she shook her head and slowly collected her things and scooted out of the booth.

Outside, she felt confused that the sun was shining brightly. People were walking along the sidewalk, entering and leaving shops nearby. None of them knew the internal nightmare that was raging through Serenity's body. Evelyn's words echoed in her mind, sharp and jarring: "The point is, he wants you. So he'll appear. For you."

"Two days," she whispered to herself, the weight of impending doom pressing down on her. Two days until she could face the monster that haunted her dreams, a grotesque specter that had already claimed Travis. Panic surged through her, hot and suffocating, and she pressed her palms against her temples, trying to will away the dread pooling in her gut.

People trying to leave the café and walk by her stared as she fought the desire to hyperventilate. What did Evelyn want? Was she truly there to help, or was she manipulating Serenity for her own gain? The questions spiraled, each one feeding her anxiety. Serenity couldn't shake the feeling that Evelyn had more knowledge than she was letting on, that there was something darker lurking beneath her well-meaning facade.

The café door swung open, and a couple of patrons stepped out, laughing and chatting, blissfully unaware of the horror lurking just beyond the edges of her consciousness. Serenity's heart sank further. They didn't know what awaited her. The darkness that loomed just around the corner.

As the vibrant life of the town continued around her, Serenity stood frozen, grappling with her fear and the uncertainty of what lay ahead. The warmth of the sun felt distant, and she couldn't shake the feeling that the shadows were closing in, a chilling prelude to the nightmare that awaited.

Eventually, Serenity swallowed down her terror and walked back to her rental car. She barely remembered her drive to the hotel, but she parked and walked inside. Desperate to be alone, she rushed through the lobby to the stairs. Inside her room, she collapsed against the door and slid to the floor.

"Travis, what am I supposed to do?" she murmured into the empty room.

As she sat against the door, exhaustion seemed to suck the energy from her body. In her confused state, she didn't even think about preventing sleep or doing any of her normal rituals. Instead, she slowly slid to the side, until she lay on the floor, her body no longer able to handle the fear that flowed through her veins.

Before long, Serenity found herself at the edge of a dense fog, her heart pounding in her chest. The air was thick with a suffocating dampness, the kind that clung to her skin and made it hard to breathe. She was no longer in her hotel room; instead, she found herself in an eerie, shadow-laden landscape, the ground beneath her shrouded in darkness.

Part of her subconscious knew that Evelyn and her explosive revelation triggered the nightmare. But the rest of her mind and body believed she was standing in the spot she and Travis launched their boat that fateful day.

"Where are you?" she called, her voice trembling as the fog swallowed her words. Panic swirled in her gut, tightening its grip as she instinctively knew what awaited her. The looming presence of Steamboat Willie lurked just beyond the veil of mist, and the thought of becoming a sacrifice sent chills through her bones. That he would return just for her caused the panic to turn to lead in her stomach.

"Serenity." The voice slithered through the fog, low and melodic, but with an undercurrent of something darker. She turned to see Evelyn standing a few paces away, her silhouette barely discernible through the haze. "You shouldn't be here alone."

"Evelyn?" Serenity felt a mix of surprise and dread. The familiar figure was a type of comfort, yet something about her presence felt twisted, distorted by the dream's oppressive atmosphere. "I'm looking for the steamboat. I have to find it before it's too late."

Evelyn stepped closer, her face obscured by shadows, but her eyes glinted with a knowing light. "You're searching in the wrong place, my dear." Her voice was soothing yet unsettling, wrapping around Serenity like a coiling vine. "You should embrace your destiny. It's not a matter of finding the steamboat, but accepting what comes next."

"What do you mean?" Serenity's voice was barely a whisper, fear flooding her senses. "I can't let him take me. I won't become a sacrifice!" The fog thickened around her, dark and heavy, pressing in on her like a stifling shroud.

Evelyn tilted her head, a smile playing on her lips that sent shivers down Serenity's spine. "Ah, but the sacrifice has already been chosen. You are the key to his return." As she spoke, the fog twisted into ghostly shapes, swirling around them and echoing the sound of distant, mocking laughter.

"Stop it!" Serenity cried, backing away, but the fog enveloped her, the world around her spinning. "I don't want this! I won't be his sacrifice! I won't give in to him!"

In a sudden flash, the ground beneath Serenity shifted, and she was transported to the edge of a murky bayou, the water black and still. The silhouette of the steamboat loomed in the distance, a monstrous shape wreathed in fog, the sound of creaking wood and distant whispers echoing in her ears. She felt an irresistible pull toward it, as if the very essence of the boat called to her soul. She could imagine Travis's soul among those that whispered to her.

"No! I won't go!" Serenity screamed, her body refusing to move as the fog thickened around her, anchoring her in place. The laughter from the steamboat grew louder, mocking and cruel, drowning out her thoughts.

As the shadows closed in, Serenity felt herself slipping away, the darkness swallowing her whole. Just as the tendrils of the fog reached out to grasp her, she screamed, a sound that reverberated through her empty hotel room—echoing into silence.

A Life for a Life

FOR TWO DAYS, SERENITY didn't leave her hotel room. She paced and didn't sleep. Her mind pushed and pulled her into different scenarios. But at the beginning of the third day, the day that everything was to align, Serenity dressed robotically. No matter her fear, she knew what she needed to do. She had to release Travis.

Standing at the edge of the bayou, Serenity tried to find the comfort she used to find in the musty warmth of nature. In the quiet that surrounded her, she could hear bugs buzzing and animals rustling through the underbrush. Randomly a splash could be heard in the river, as turtles, fish, and birds moved throughout the ecosystem.

Behind her, a car pulled in, and Serenity's spine stiffened. Turning, she found a small SUV towing a rowboat that looked brand new. Evelyn was behind the wheel, and she didn't acknowledge Serenity as she expertly turned and backed the trailer into the water. Jumping from the car, Evelyn got the rowboat off the trailer and tied to a small dock before pulling the trailer back out of the water.

Evelyn was dressed similarly to Serenity, wearing sturdy boots, cargo pants, and a T-shirt with a flannel over it. She had a backpack slung over one shoulder and her gray hair was pulled into a severe bun. Her eyes were hidden behind sunglasses, but Serenity could feel the heat of her stare as she approached.

"You showed." Evelyn's words were a statement of fact, no hint of surprise or doubt.

"My options were limited."

Serenity lifted her own backpack and followed Evelyn toward the dock. The older woman glanced over her shoulder once and inspected Serenity. "What's in the bag?"

"My own supplies." She wasn't willing to tell Evelyn everything she had or was willing to use to destroy Willie. Whatever the woman's intentions were, Serenity wasn't sure she could trust they were what was best for her.

Evelyn accepted the answer with a shrug, and when they got to the boat, she tossed her own bag in. Serenity held tight to hers, while her free hand rubbed at the evil eye that was under her shirt. Ember hadn't given her specific instructions, but she felt safest with the cool gold against her heated skin.

She was also not sharing with Evelyn that she had done another smudging of herself in her hotel room that morning. Serenity had wanted to believe that Ember knew what she was talking about as she let the smoke waft around her. She imagined any evil lingering on her body, dissipating with the smoke. No matter her beliefs, the ritual made Serenity feel lighter and more prepared for what they might face in the bayou.

Evelyn immediately took up position at the small motor at the back of the boat. They had oars, with the chance they needed to row, but that would take much longer. The engine came to life with a small sputter, and soon they were moving away from the dock. The sound was loud in Serenity's ears, echoing through the cypress trees that formed a canopy over their heads.

As they slid through the water, the sunny day seemed to darken. Serenity lifted her gaze from the dark expanse around them, finding an unnatural fog beginning to roll in. Ahead of the boat, she could see the familiar bend in the river that she knew she had only seen in her dreams since Travis disappeared.

"Are you ready?" Evelyn's voice cut through the fog, but there was an unsettling calmness to her demeanor. Serenity felt a shiver of doubt as she glanced at the woman who had seemed like an ally but now appeared shrouded in darkness. She had pushed her sunglasses to the top of her head and was staring ahead toward the bend in the river.

"I have to find Travis," Serenity whispered, her heart pounding in her chest. She turned forward, feeling drawn deeper into the bayou, away from the safety of the dock and her life after Willie. "He needs me."

The engine was the only noise as they approached the bend. A cold sweat beaded along Serenity's hairline, droplets sliding down her neck. A voice inside her head encouraged her to close her eyes, squeeze them tight, to not see what she knew they would find. She felt the boat speed up, the engine whining under the pressure Evelyn was putting on it. The woman was desperate to approach their potential death.

The air was thick with humidity as Serenity and Evelyn moved through the winding waterways of the bayou. The sound of their engine slicing through the still water echoed in the eerie silence. Towering cypress trees draped in Spanish moss loomed overhead, their gnarled branches reaching out like skeletal fingers. Serenity's heart raced with each stroke, a mixture of fear and determination propelling her forward.

"Just around this bend," Evelyn said, her voice steady but tinged with an undercurrent of anticipation. Serenity glanced at her, catching a glimpse of resolve etched on the older woman's face, yet there was a flicker of something darker in her eyes—an intensity that made Serenity's pulse quicken. There was more to this story.

As they rounded the bend that Serenity wanted nothing more than to run from, the fog seemed to thicken and swirl ominously. Out of the water, it appeared, as if conjured, just for them to happen upon. There was no sound, no creaking, no animals or insects. The bayou had gone silent as the evil appeared.

"There it is," Evelyn breathed.

The steamboat was just as Serenity remembered. A once grand vessel, decaying and sinking into the bayou's dark waters. It was a dark hulking shape, cloaked in darkness and evil, moss hanging from each floor. The sight stole Serenity's breath.

Evelyn slowed the boat, angling it to come alongside the decrepit vessel.

Serenity felt a chill run down her spine, and she swallowed hard, forcing herself to look away from the imposing vessel. "We have to be careful," she warned, her heart racing. "This place...it feels wrong."

As they boarded the steamboat, the atmosphere shifted, the shadows deepening around them. Serenity felt an inexplicable pull toward the depths of the vessel, where whispers of lost souls echoed like a haunting melody. "Travis!" she called out, her voice trembling.

Memories assailed her, taking her back to that day. She was a teenager again, exploring the strange boat, laughing and feeling joy with her best friend. As they crept down the deck, she stopped at the hole she fell into. Without seeing the bottom, she knew it was full of water.

Suddenly, a flicker of light appeared in the darkness—a figure emerged, translucent and glowing, a familiar silhouette. "Serenity..." It was Travis, his expression filled with sorrow and longing. Relief washed over her, but a wave of desperation quickly replaced it.

"Travis! I'm here! I'm going to free you!" Serenity cried, reaching out toward him. But as she approached, the air grew colder, and Travis's form flickered like a candle in the wind.

"Help me," he pleaded, his voice wavering. "You have to stop him."

Before she could respond, Evelyn stepped forward, a twisted smile curling on her lips. "You're not the only one who has lost someone, Serenity. My son disappeared in these waters. My Jonas. I thought he might still be alive, trapped like Travis. It was Willie who took him. He has the power to return them, to bring my son back."

Serenity stared at her, the truth hitting her like a sledgehammer. She filtered through her memory of the day in the library, trying to see if she missed any signs or information that would have led to this revelation. "That's crazy, Evelyn. Travis is dead. If your son was taken by Willie, he's dead too."

Evelyn turned toward Serenity. It was then she noticed that the woman was holding a large hunting knife. Serenity stepped back, but that put her at the edge of the gaping black hole in the decking.

"You aren't the only one who has had dreams. Willie has come to me too," Evelyn said, as she stepped forward. "A life for a life. That's what he told me. Bringing you here is what he demanded, for my son's life."

The Last
Goodbye

"Evelyn, you can't do this!" Serenity shouted, a knot of dread tightening in her stomach as the realization of Evelyn's intentions hit her. "Travis is gone. Your son is gone. You can't sacrifice me to bring back someone who may not even be here!"

Evelyn's eyes darkened, her desperation morphing into something malevolent. "You're wrong. You are the key to releasing them both. It's time for you to fulfill your purpose!"

Before Serenity could react, Evelyn lunged at her, the movement swift and predatory. Serenity dodged the knife, leaping to the side and avoiding falling into the hole. The two women struggled, the steamboat creaking ominously beneath them. Serenity's instincts kicked in as she fought back, pushing Evelyn away. "I won't let you do this!"

The boat shuddered violently, and a deep, rumbling laughter echoed from the shadows. Steamboat Willie materialized, moving through the moss, his grotesque form looming over them, eyes glinting with hunger. "Another soul for my collection," he sneered, his voice dripping with malice.

Serenity was slammed back into her nightmares as she stared at Willie. His decaying body did not differ from the first time she had seen him. The ripped overalls, hanging off his body, the name tag the only thing showing he may have been a human man at some point. His oversized head, with a razor-sharp smile, was turned toward Serenity. If she didn't know any better, she would swear there was a light of recognition in his expression. His sunken, hollow eye sockets were locked on her.

Behind Willie, she could still see Travis, his ethereal form stuck in the teenage body he had died in. He didn't look the way he had in some of Serenity's dreams. As a ghost, his skin lacked the youthful glow, but he was whole without injury or blood. His eyes were bright and fearful as he watched Serenity and Evelyn.

"Stay back!" Serenity shouted, feeling the raw energy of fear coursing through her veins. With a burst of adrenaline, she pushed past Evelyn and raced toward Travis's ghost, determination igniting within her. "I'll free you! I promise!"

"Serenity, no!" Evelyn cried, her voice laced with desperation. "You'll only make it worse! We need to make the sacrifice!" She tried to grab hold of her.

But Serenity could feel the chains of despair that bound Travis, and in that moment, she understood what she had to do. "I'll set you free!" she yelled, turning to face Evelyn, her resolve solidifying. The woman had lied to her, used her, and brought her to the steamboat as a sacrifice.

With a swift motion, Serenity pulled out a bag of salt she had put in her pocket before she ever got on Evelyn's boat. Remembering Ember's words, she quickly spun, creating a circle around herself. Willie seemed to take a step back, his oversized head tilting to the side, taking in what was happening. She turned to face Evelyn, who had regained her footing and was advancing, eyes wild with desperation.

"You want a sacrifice? Here!" Serenity shouted, her voice strong and unwavering. She grabbed the pendant that hung around her neck and thrust it toward Willie, channeling all her energy and intention into it. "Take her!"

The pendant glowed brightly, a beacon of light cutting through the shadows. In that moment, Evelyn's expression shifted from determination to horror as the shadows coiled around her, pulling her toward Willie. "No! Serenity, you can't!" she screamed, but it was too late.

Willie's laughter echoed as he reached for Evelyn, the dark energy swirling around them. Serenity felt a surge of power wash over her, and as the shadows engulfed Evelyn, a burst of energy erupted from the pendant, creating a barrier that pushed Serenity back. She stumbled, but kept herself on her feet, wondering for a brief second what Ember had done to the pendant. The insistence that she wore it painted a clear picture of what she believed was coming for Serenity.

Travis's ghost flickered, his expression shifting from despair to hope. "Thank you," he whispered, and in that moment, Serenity felt a profound sense of relief. The air grew lighter, the shadows retreating as Evelyn was consumed by the darkness of the steamboat.

With a final, piercing scream, Evelyn disappeared into the shadows, and the laughter faded into silence. The steamboat shuddered, its power waning as the oppressive energy lifted.

Travis stepped forward, his form brightening as the darkness receded. "You did it, Ser. You freed me," he said, a radiant light enveloping him. He was the boy she had loved so dearly, and she committed his face to memory.

Tears streamed down Serenity's face, a mix of relief and grief. "I'm so sorry," she whispered, knowing the weight of their journey. But she could feel the warmth of his presence, the bond they shared transcending the darkness.

Travis disappeared into a brightness that Serenity could only hope to join him in someday. After she had lived a long, beautiful life. His smile faded, and his hand lifted, as if waving goodbye.

"Goodbye, my friend." Serenity knew she wouldn't have nightmares of him again.

The steamboat structure shook violently, nearly knocking Serenity off her feet. She grabbed her backpack, which had fallen during her struggle with Evelyn, and ran to the side of the boat where the rowboat was tied. With shaking fingers, she untied the rope and quickly climbed back into the small rowboat. Using an oar, she pushed away from the steamboat as it continued to ripple with movement.

Just as she got the engine running on the boat, she turned and watched as the steamboat seemed to fold in on itself until nothing was left but the cypress trees and Spanish moss. The water barely moved in the spot, and the bayou life began to sing once again. Serenity sat in shock, waiting for something else to happen. She didn't know how long she waited, but as the sun disappeared, she knew she needed to get back to her car before dark.

The heavy weight of Travis's death was no longer sitting like a stone in her heart. No longer would her last memory of him be his broken and bleeding form, saving her from a monster. She could now feel comfort knowing he had gone to a place much more beautiful and serene than where he had been since his death.

Later, in her rental car, she drove to the Witching Willow. She needed to tell Ember what had happened and how the pendant had protected her. A thank you was on the tip of her tongue, even if she didn't understand what had happened. She bumped along the gravel road, her headlights guiding the way. When the light flashed across the front of the shop, Serenity felt confusion swirl in her mind.

Parking so her headlights lit up the cabin, she slowly approached the building. If she hadn't followed the same GPS and just been there a few days before, she would have sworn she was in the wrong place. Boards covered the cabin windows. There was a thick layer of dust across the porch and railing. Moss hung in the places that chimes and pendants had.

Serenity approached, pushing through the moss to find the front door. Trying the knob, she found it locked. Using her cellphone flashlight, she peered between the boards on the front windows. Expecting to see bookcases full of products, she stumbled back when all she found was an empty cabin. Old graffiti covered the inside walls, marking where someone had broken in and had their fun.

Her movement was stilted as she walked back off the porch and found her way to her car. Again, she double-checked her GPS and her location on the map. She was in the right place. But the Witching Willow wasn't there. And it hadn't been in a very long time.

Breaking the Chains

FALLING ASLEEP AND HAVING dreams no longer scared Serenity. When Travis visited her at night, it was never at the steamboat. She never saw Willie again in her nightmares. The witch bottle Ember had gifted her was tucked under her mattress, and she wasn't willing to tempt fate by removing it. She also continued to wear the evil eye over her heart, where it made her feel safe.

For a few days after the encounter with Steamboat Willie, Serenity had continued to stay in her hotel and spent time wandering the area. She was hoping to find an answer about who Ember was. All she could find out was that she had indeed been the owner of the Witching Willow, but people were mixed about when that was. Serenity had to wonder if Ember had appeared to others in need, confusing the town about her existence.

When she finally drove home to Georgia, she said a small prayer to the Wiccan woman. Something in her heart told her that Ember was a natural enemy of evil and when Serenity stumbled upon the Witching Willow, she knew her need. It explained the strange way Ember looked at her, as she read her, knowing everything that was happening inside her mind. In the end, that connection saved Serenity's life and freed Travis from his purgatory.

Ember wasn't the only unanswered question Serenity had. The disappearance of the steamboat and Willie taking Evelyn as a sacrifice didn't confirm that the monster would never come back. Serenity took the absence of her nightmares as a sign that her connection to the demon was severed. However, what of Evelyn?

She could avoid the curiosity for a few years. Until one day, she looked up the local news in her hometown. Keeping track of the measurements Evelyn had said needed to line up for Willie to appear, Serenity had a good idea of when the steamboat might haunt the bayou again. The headline in the local newspaper sent chills down her spine. Two men, missing, when they didn't return from a fishing trip on the bayou. They had launched their boat from the same place Serenity and Travis had.

Serenity stared at the website and felt that familiar fear tug at her stomach. Even without the nightmares, she could remember every grotesque detail of Willie. His skeletal shape, oversized head, with large ears. The razor-sharp teeth lining his mouth, that you could see clearly when he smiled at you. And the name tag, hanging precariously from the destroyed overalls, looking as if it would fall off at any moment.

Gripping the evil eye at her neck, she rubbed the stone as she had done daily since freeing Travis. She shook her head as if she could will away the reality that lingered. She had fought against the darkness, and in her heart, she believed Willie was gone, banished by her will and the light of her determination, with the help of the power Ember had infused her with. The laughter of the demon had faded, replaced by the silence of the bayou, but a lingering doubt clung to her thoughts.

She had the unreasonable desire to call Daphne and tell her what she had found. But, no, she couldn't bother her best friend with this.She was too busy as a happily married woman with her first baby on the way.Serenity never begrudged her the chance at a wonderfully happy life, something she hoped to have herself someday. But she did miss the companionship. She reminded herself that she was an adult, capable of living on her own.

As she continued to read, the details of the article blurred into the background, her mind racing with memories of the horrors she had faced. A sudden chill swept through the room, the warmth of the sunlight dimming as if a shadow had passed over her. Serenity's heart quickened, an instinctive awareness prickling at the back of her neck. Her grip on the evil eye tightened, and she pictured the jar of ceremonial salt that she kept on the counter of the kitchen. It was a habit she just couldn't break.

Then it came—an echoing sound that sent shivers through her body. The unmistakable, sinister laughter of Steamboat Willie rang out, rich and mocking, reverberating through the walls of her home. Serenity froze, her breath hitching in her throat as she looked around, wide-eyed and disbelieving.

"No..." she breathed, the reality crashing down on her. "He can't be here. It's over."

But the laughter continued, wrapping around her like a dark fog, seeping into her thoughts. Panic surged within her as she shot up from the chair, her heart racing. The sound was all too familiar, a chilling reminder of the terror she thought she had escaped.

She glanced back at the laptop screen, her pulse pounding in her ears. The article lay open, the faces of the missing men haunting her. A deep sense of dread settled in her stomach as she realized that this laughter wasn't just a figment of her imagination; it was a portent, a reminder that evil could never truly be banished. A monster continued to haunt the bayou, feasting on those who lived near the water.

The laughter abruptly cut off, replaced by a suffocating silence that enveloped her. Serenity stood there, her heart racing, the tension in the air palpable. Had she truly banished him? Or was this just a lull before the storm?

The shadow that darkened the room slowly lifted, and the sun shone into her home again. Serenity fought hard for the light she lived in. The battle against evil had been fought, and she had accomplished what she sought to do. Now, the memory lingered like a death shroud, reminding her of what existed in the world.

She understood now that true strength wasn't merely about vanquishing evil, but about confronting it head-on, acknowledging its presence without letting it consume her. With each breath, she committed to embracing the light she fought so hard to reclaim, to sew her experiences into a tapestry of resilience. Serenity knew that while Willie's darkness would always be a part of her story, it would not define her. She would carry the weight of that knowledge, not as a burden but as a testament to her strength—forever vigilant, forever brave, ready to face whatever shadows may come.

Twisted Tales of Familiar Faces

If you enjoyed this corrupted retelling of *Steamboat Willie*, don't miss out on the rest of this horrifying collection!

Humbug (Scrooge) - Andre Gonzalez

Sweethaven (Popeye) - RJ Clark

Timber Beast (Paul Bunyan) - A.K. Hughey

Alice (Alice in Wonderland) - Audrey Brice

Wish (Aladdin) - Courtney Konstantin

Quixote (Don Quixote) - Stephen Wertzbaugher

Arturius (King Arthur) - A.K. Hughey

Steamboat (Steamboat Willie) - Courtney Konstantin

Strangled (Rapunzel) - Stephen Wertzbaugher

Dethroning Oz (Wizard of Oz) - Audrey Brice

Scorned (Hercules) - Z.S. Diamanti

Check out the entire collection at www.m4lpublishing.com

Join our newsletter to stay up to date with all upcoming releases at www.m4lpublishing.com

Author's Note

Thank you for reading Steamboat, a Twisted Tales of Familiar Faces novella.

Firstly, my appreciation goes to M4L Publishing, especially Andre and Natasha. Thank you for inviting me to be a part of the Twisted Tales Series. Your faith in my work has been an enormous encouragement.

To my fellow Twisted Tales authors, thank you for your camaraderie and collaboration. Staying connected about the series has been invaluable. Your creativity and enthusiasm have made this journey all the more enjoyable. (Except you Stephen...you know what you did. haha)

A special thanks to my TWS team for your unwavering support and dedication. Your encouragement and belief in my vision have been pillars of strength throughout this process.

To my family—my incredible husband and wonderful children: thank you for your love, support, and for the sacrifices you make that allow me the time and space to pursue my passion for storytelling. You are my inspiration and motivation, and without your support, this book would not have been possible.

Enjoy this book?

We hope you enjoyed this release from M4L Publishing.

Reviews are the most helpful tools in getting new readers for any books. We don't have the financial backing of a New York publishing house and can't afford to blast our books on billboards or bus stops.

(Not yet!)

That said, your honest review can go a long way in helping us reach new readers. If you've enjoyed this book, we'd be forever grateful if you could spend a couple minutes leaving it a review (it can be as short as you like) on the site you purchased this book from.

Thank you so much!

About the author

A Northern California native now settled in Oregon, Courtney is a writer fascinated by apocalyptic tales and the unraveling of societal norms. She finds joy in hiking, reading, exploring new destinations—especially cruises—and savoring time with family, all of which inspire her stories of resilience and survival.